A smear of bright .... t to
Longarm's right, a .... un-
tainside high to th...

"Son of a *bitch* .... behind the boulder he'd been sitting on. He'd taken cover
almost without thought, and by the time he got behind the
boulder he had his Colt in his hand and his Stetson off
so it would not serve as a marker for the distant rifleman
to shoot at.

Longarm moved a little to his left so he could remain
under cover but get a better angle of view toward where
he suspected the gunman might be.

For more than a minute he neither saw nor heard anything. Then there was a puff of smoke at the base of a
scrub oak about thirty feet to the right of where he'd been
looking.

He saw the wisp of smoke. Heard a slug impact the
ground some fifteen feet to Longarm's left. Finally heard
the rifle shot itself.

Longarm frowned. The first bullet struck a good ten
feet to his right. Now this one hit at least that far to his
left.

This was no assassination attempt. Whoever was up
there was deliberately aiming wide. Either that or the bastard was the worst marksman in the history of humankind.

Longarm stood up in plain view and with deliberate
care shoved his Colt back into its cross-draw holster so
the rifleman could see what he was doing.

No third gunshot followed, further convincing Longarm
that he was right about this. That bastard with the rifle
didn't want to shoot him. He wanted to scare him away.

Perhaps this was his idea of fair warning.

If so, he was going to be badly disappointed. It would
take more than threats to move Custis Long off the trail
of a murderer. . . .

DON'T MISS THESE
ALL-ACTION WESTERN SERIES
FROM THE BERKLEY PUBLISHING GROUP

THE GUNSMITH by J. R. Roberts
Clint Adams was a legend among lawmen, outlaws, and ladies. They called him . . . the Gunsmith.

LONGARM by Tabor Evans
The popular long-running series about U.S. Deputy Marshal Long—his life, his loves, his fight for justice.

SLOCUM by Jake Logan
Today's longest-running action Western. John Slocum rides a deadly trail of hot blood and cold steel.

BUSHWHACKERS by B. J. Lanagan
An action-packed series by the creators of Longarm! The rousing adventures of the most brutal gang of cutthroats ever assembled—Quantrill's Raiders.

DIAMONDBACK by Guy Brewer
Dex Yancey is Diamondback, a southern gentleman turned con man when his brother cheats him out of the family fortune. Ladies love him. Gamblers hate him. But nobody pulls one over on Dex . . .

WILDGUN by Jack Hanson
Will Barlow's continuing search for his daughter, kidnapped by the Blackfeet Indians who slaughtered the rest of his family.

TABOR EVANS

LONGARM

AND THE
MOUNTAIN BANDIT

JOVE BOOKS, NEW YORK

LONGARM AND THE MOUNTAIN BANDIT

A Jove Book / published by arrangement with
the author

PRINTING HISTORY
Jove edition / February 2001

All rights reserved.
Copyright © 2001 by Penguin Putnam Inc.
This book, or parts thereof, may not be reproduced in any form
without permission.
For information address: The Berkley Publishing Group,
a division of Penguin Putnam Inc.,
375 Hudson Street, New York, New York 10014.

The Penguin Putnam Inc. World Wide Web site address is
http://www.penguinputnam.com

ISBN: 0-515-13018-4

A JOVE BOOK®
Jove Books are published by The Berkley Publishing Group,
a division of Penguin Putnam Inc.,
375 Hudson Street, New York, New York 10014.
JOVE and the "J" design
are trademarks belonging to Penguin Putnam Inc.

PRINTED IN THE UNITED STATES OF AMERICA

10 9 8 7 6 5 4 3 2 1

Chapter 1

Longarm crossed his legs and dipped two fingers into his vest pocket to retrieve his watch and check the time. Eleven-eleven and counting. It was unlike the boss to be late. Billy Vail had said to be there at eleven, and Longarm hadn't been more than two or three minutes late. That might well be a record. So where the hell was Billy?

Not that it mattered, Longarm supposed. They would go over next week's assignments and then, with any kind of luck, Longarm would be free to spend this Friday afternoon on his own.

It was a gloriously beautiful summer day, and Denver was alive with the smell of fresh-cut grass and blooming flowers. A perfect day for a walk in the park.

Longarm didn't generally spend his free time walking in parks. But today he hoped to make an exception. There was a young lady who'd moved into the boardinghouse three doors down from his, and it was her habit to stroll in the public park that stretched along the banks of Cherry Creek.

If Custis Long should just happen to meet her there, why, there was no telling where a budding relationship might lead. And this *was* the season for plants and things to blossom, was it not? He hoped so.

Longarm yawned and checked his watch again. Elevenfourteen and still no Billy. This was becoming annoying. The young lady in question liked to walk in the early afternoons, immediately after lunch, and Longarm wanted time to get a quick haircut and splash of Pinaud scent before he took his own little sojourn in the sunshine.

He stood and paced for a few minutes, then stopped in front of the mirror and coat tree that sat off to the side of the United States marshal's office.

His dark brown hair and full mustache really could use a trim. They weren't shaggy. Exactly. But he could definitely use a trim if he wanted to show himself to best advantage.

Not that Longarm considered that he had so very much to show off. He thought of himself as ordinary, even plain. Fortunately, a good many ladies seemed to think otherwise.

He stood over six feet tall and had a horseman's lean build with a flat belly, narrow hips, and broad shoulders. His face was more craggy and chiseled than smooth or handsome, and his skin was burnt brown from frequent exposure to the elements.

He had brown eyes, dark brown hair, and tended to dress in browns as well. Brown tweed coat. Brown calfskin vest. Pale brown corduroy trousers. Dark brown Stetson hat. His leather, however, he liked in black. Black stovepipe cavalry boots. Black gunbelt and cross-draw holster.

And a heavy gold watch chain suspended between his vest pockets, at one end of which was the usual watch. The casual observer would likely not suspect that the other end of the chain held not a fob, but a brass-framed derringer pistol in .44 caliber.

Longarm gave himself a critical inspection, used the heels of both hands to smooth down the hair over his ears where the Stetson had rumpled it, then paced some more until finally—he resisted an impulse to take his watch out and check the time yet again—the door opened and the U.S. marshal for the Denver District walked in.

" 'Lo, Billy."

"Hello, Deputy." Longarm was not particularly pleased with the form of greeting. To call him Longarm or even Custis would be friendly and casual. To call him by title . . . that was official. Longarm really didn't want official right now. Today he'd have been happier with a casual chat and then that stroll. And never mind the visit to his barber on the way home. It was getting too late for that.

"Henry tells me you were almost on time," Billy said.

"Yes, sir."

Vail hurried into his chair and plunked himself into it. He looked like an aging, mousy filing clerk with a bald dome, round red face, and innocent blue eyes. Longarm happened to know that William Vail was about as innocent as a whorehouse piano player. The man had been a Texas Ranger before securing his appointment as marshal, and he was death on the hoof with a six-gun. Appearances did at times deceive.

"Sorry I'm later than I expected," Vail said. "I had to go over to the postmaster's office."

"Special-delivery receipts? I thought Henry was authorized to accept documents."

"Nothing to do with the receipt of warrants and writs this time," Vail said. "The postmaster has a problem. And so do we now that he's asked us to handle the investigation."

"What happened to all those postal inspectors he's so proud of?" Longarm asked. He already knew the answer, of course. The Post Office's supposed enforcement arm was stacked, in this district at least, with political appointees, men the postmaster owed for past favors, or worse, men whose fathers, uncles, or cousins were owed favors. The relatives of political hacks were the worst of the worst. Most of them probably had difficulty figuring out which end to wipe after their morning shit.

"Don't get me started," Billy said.

Longarm shut his mouth and took out a cheroot to fiddle with. He knew better than to light it in the office. Billy

3

was on some sort of health kick and had developed a sudden distaste for the smell of a fine cigar. But Custis could at least get it ready to light. And maybe chew on it a little.

"There's been a string of mail robberies," Billy said. "They started back in February. Seems the mail between the Fairplay and Alma district across to Leadville has been held up on the first carry of every month since then."

"And the postmaster is just now getting around to noticing it?" Longarm injected. "Quick on the uptake, that man."

"I gather he thought even his dullards could handle the robberies since they know who was pulling them."

Longarm raised an eyebrow but did not interrupt again.

"That was until earlier this week. One of the postal inspectors was shot dead while engaged in his official investigation."

"I see. That kinda makes it serious, doesn't it?"

"Damned serious. It also puts our postmaster and his people in way over their heads. The only good thing is that at least now he recognizes the fact."

"I don't suppose you mentioned to him that his man would likely still be alive now if he'd let professionals handle this from the get-go," Longarm said.

"I didn't have to, Custis. He said it himself. Although I'm not sure if his grief has to do with the loss of the man, or if it's because of the reaction from the dead man's family. They are, shall we say, highly influential in certain, ahem, elevated circles."

"Political ass-lickers," Longarm said dryly.

"I did not say that, did I?"

"No, Boss, but you damn sure thought it. Same as I did."

"Yes, well, all that is irrelevant. What we have now are a very dead government employee and a deep and burning desire to apprehend the killer of same."

"And I take it I'm the one gonna do the apprehending?" Billy nodded.

"You said a little while ago that the postmaster already knew who the robber was. Can we assume the killer and the robber are one and the same?"

"We probably shouldn't count on that assumption, Longarm, but we certainly should use that as our starting point."

"Yes, sir."

"Henry is making some excerpts from the postmaster's records about the robberies. Also a little about the dead postal inspector. He should have those ready for you to pick up immediately after lunch."

"Yes, sir."

"You'll have plenty of time to make the three-seventeen to Fairplay."

"Yes, sir."

So much for lazy summer afternoons and strolling in the park.

But then those things weren't the reason they were paying him a United States deputy marshal's wage.

Longarm jammed the unlighted cheroot between his teeth and bent to pluck his hat from the floor, where he'd dropped it when he came in.

"I will expect full and frequent reports, Longarm," Billy reminded him.

Longarm grinned at his boss. "Yes, sir. You always do."

The boss at least had enough sense of humor in him to make a sour face and shake his head sadly.

He always wanted full and frequent reports from his deputies in the field.

He damned seldom got them, especially from Deputy Custis Long.

Longarm eased out of Billy's office and headed for a quick lunch. There were a good many things he needed to do before he left, including picking up his laundry so he could restock his always ready traveling bag. Always ready, that is, except for today.

Chapter 2

Longarm propped his feet on the soot-grimed seat of the bench across from his in the rattletrap smoker car. For some reason—perhaps on the theory that smokers wouldn't be bothered by a little extra smoke—they always put the smoking car close behind the engine and tender where the thick smoke from the coal-fired boilers was sure to fill the air and make the simple act of breathing a great accomplishment.

Cinders blew in with the billowing, suffocating smoke, and a man had to be careful lest a live one mar his clothes with pea-sized burn holes. Hell, Longarm had even seen a man once who'd had only half a mustache. He'd fallen asleep in the smoker car, and a particularly large clinker had landed in his mustache and set the hair on fire. Longarm hadn't been willing to nod off in the smoking car ever since, insisting instead on walking back to a regular passenger coach if he wanted to take a nap.

There'd be no napping today, though. Certainly not while there was still enough daylight to let him get some reading in. He'd brought along a pasteboard folio with a string closure that Henry had prepared for him earlier.

Billy Vail's secretary had, as usual, been thorough. There were five robbery reports for the holdups from

February through June, plus an offense record for the felon thought to be both robber and now murderer. Henry hadn't copied out the reports in full, of course, as his time had been limited, but Longarm knew he could trust Henry to have put down all the important points in these excerpts.

They were all written out, not in longhand, but with one of those mechanical typing devices. Henry claimed the odd little machines were actually faster than handwriting. And maybe they were. For Henry or someone else who knew how to use one. Damned if anybody would ever catch Longarm poking at those funny little round tabs, though. He couldn't make heads nor tails out of the gadgets.

He sat there for quite some time with a cold and forgotten cheroot in one hand and Henry's folio in his lap while he pored over one typewritten sheet after another.

The robbery reports all seemed fairly ordinary. And with no mystery about them. The postman on the Fairplay-Alma-to-Leadville route had no options as to the road he would take. There was only one.

The road from Alma climbed to Mosquito Pass at the summit of the Mosquito Range, then wound its way down to the Arkansas River valley close to its headwaters above Leadville.

Once down to the river level, a traveler again had only one road to take, although at least then he had two choices. He could go upstream to Leadville, or he could turn down and follow the river through Buena Vista and Texas Creek to Canon City and finally out onto the plains. By then the Arkansas River was no longer the narrow, fast-running creek he would have found high in the mountains near Leadville, but a broad, surging river that dominated much of the southern plains.

In any event, with the mail carrier's route limited to only that one road, all a robber need do was decide which of the thousand or more turns, cutbacks, aspen stands, or boulders he wanted to lurk behind, then wait for his victim to come to him.

Finding his victim under circumstances like that offered about as much suspense and excitement as hunting hogs in a sty.

Each time he struck, the robber chose a different hiding place, but each time the method was the same.

Wearing a mask made out of a flour sack turned inside out and decorated with a leering face drawn in charcoal, the robber would simply step out into the road with his double-barreled scattergun cocked and leveled.

A few mute motions were enough to convey the message.

Once the mail carrier dropped his mailbag, the robber would step aside and ceremoniously take the shotgun hammers down to half cock. Then he'd motion for the postman to proceed.

Never in all the five robberies had a single word been exchanged between the robber and the postman.

Naturally there was no way to know if the man had had words with the postal inspector who'd been assigned to catch him. The inspector, a man named Fitz Barrington, did not live long enough to write any reports on his progress, if there'd been any.

The day he died he'd told the letter carrier, a man named Ed Macklin, that he shouldn't worry because he, Barrington, would follow along behind and would arrest the robber once he'd shown himself.

Macklin later reported that he was held up on that trip near the notch where the road crossed Mosquito Pass from the Platte River drainage on the east slope of the mountain into the Arkansas River drainage on the western side of the pass.

Macklin said the robber appeared by surprise, as usual, and motioned for the mail pouch, which Macklin immediately dropped. The robber waved him on, and Macklin went ahead on his route as he always did. He had to continue, so he could make the back-haul later in the week from Leadville to Fairplay-Alma.

His route was three days out and three days back again, week in and week out.

On the date of the June robbery he obeyed the robber's silent commands and then went on. He hadn't seen Fitz Barrington since leaving the way station that morning, and could not say with any degree of certainty whether the postal inspector was still trailing him or not.

He neither heard nor saw anything of interest, he said, after he left the robber near the pass. He heard no gunshots and saw nothing at all suspicious.

Barrington's body was found lying in plain sight in the middle of the road, almost dead center inside Mosquito Pass. He'd been shot at close range with a shotgun. Shot in the stomach and again, from much closer range, in the face. The killer had been thorough if nothing else. The first shot surely would have killed Barrington, but after the finishing shot that carried most of the skull away, there was no room for doubt.

Fitz Barrington had found the robber just as he'd predicted he would. Only the outcome had departed from the postal inspector's plan.

The killer was a cold and deadly son of a bitch, Longarm reminded himself before he turned to the portion of the report devoted to the prime—and only—suspect.

The suspect—Longarm reminded himself that the man was supposed to be considered only a suspect at this point and never mind the rest of the facts—was a thirty-nine-year-old gent who'd spent roughly half his life in the federal penal facility at Fort Leavenworth, Kansas.

He'd been confined there for—what a coincidence—grand larceny. Specifically, he'd stolen mail. Robbed a post office in Great Bend, Kansas, and gotten away with $387, mostly in stamps. He'd also taken a bag of mail that he opened and presumably found cash in, although he burned the mail after rifling it, and never confessed to how much if any additional money he might have found in the first-class mail.

Charles Ellis had been seventeen when he was convicted of that theft and sentenced to a term of twenty years to life at Leavenworth. On the recommendation of the warden, he was granted release at the expiration of the minimum twenty-year incarceration and was returned to society.

Ellis was reported to have come west to Denver and then into the mountains after his release from prison two years back. His last known address had been Alma, Colorado, where he was employed at the Reed Brothers silver diggings.

His current whereabouts were unknown, at least to Henry. A note attached to the synopsis of Ellis's criminal career promised more details as soon as Henry could secure information from the prison in Leavenworth.

One added bit of information Henry had already been able to establish, though, was that when sentenced, young Ellis had shouted obscenities and, among other things, vowed to kill the judge who imposed the sentence and wreak vengeance on the United States Post Office.

The opinion in at least some circles now was that a freed and embittered Ellis was doing his best to make good on those vows.

Longarm read through the reports once quickly, then more slowly a second time.

Interesting, he thought.

But there was an awful lot yet to be learned.

With daylight fading and a long way yet to climb, Longarm finished a last cheroot and then made his way back through the rattling, swaying cars to the passenger coach where he'd left his things under the very helpful eyes of a very pretty young woman.

She hadn't volunteered to watch them exactly, but she'd smiled mighty pretty when he suggested it. And she had dimples. He did most thoroughly like dimples.

11

Chapter 3

Dimples. Darn girl showed them to him again just after Longarm handed her down from the hissing, rumbling train onto the platform outside Fairplay.

And just before she introduced him to her husband, who was short, fat, ugly, and damn-all lucky to've landed himself such a fine-looking filly to keep his house and cook his food and do whatever else it was that she did for him.

"Dear, this is United States Deputy Marshal Custis Long. Marshal, this is my husband, Alexander Dumont. Alex is superintendent of the Lucky Dog mine." The dimples appeared again. She seemed proud of her man. Far as Longarm could see, it was Alex Dumont and not some hole in the ground that was the lucky dog around there.

"My pleasure, Marshal. May we offer you a ride into town?"

"I wouldn't want to put you out."

"No trouble at all really. The carriage is here and there's more than room enough for you."

For reasons known only to God and some long-forgotten railroad engineers, the railroad to Fairplay did not go to Fairplay. Instead, there was a depot on a gravel flat overlooking the headwaters of the South Platte River about a mile and a half from the town.

And at that it wasn't half as bad as the Santa Fe line, which in fact didn't go anywhere close to Santa Fe. Instead the nearest railway to the New Mexico territorial capital was at Lamy some dozen-and-a-half rough wagon miles from Santa Fe, and never the hell mind what they chose to name the railroad.

Here at Fairplay, the name of the town was likewise ignored by the hack and freight drivers who were sure to meet every scheduled passenger train. Transportation over that very short distance cost a man an arm and a leg. Or fifty cents, whichever he wanted to contribute. Longarm generally walked it on those occasions when he found himself traveling here.

"If you're sure it would be no bother," Longarm said, consenting to the man's generous offer.

"It would be our pleasure," young Mrs. Dumont assured him.

She was traveling with enough luggage for three men and a boy. Which probably meant that by female standards she'd packed mighty light. Must've been gone for only a day or two, Longarm thought as he watched two sturdy young men swing into motion to quickly retrieve the lady's baggage and load it into the back of a very handsome brougham.

Longarm managed to lift his own gear. It included only two items: a commodious and much-worn old carpetbag and an equally well-used McClellan saddle with a Winchester carbine and scabbard attached.

He tossed his items into the luggage boot on top of Mrs. Dumont's trunks and hat cases and whatnot, then helped the lady into the brougham and assisted her husband up the metal step also. Longarm trailed the pair of lovebirds.

"Have you visited Fairplay before, Marshal?" Dumont asked.

"Yes, sir, in the line of duty a time or two." He'd been

here once of his own accord too, but that was a memory too painful to reflect back on and a subject he tried to avoid as completely as possible.

"Have you a preference as to hotel?"

"Last time I was here, sir, there weren't many choices available. Only the Fairplay Hotel and a couple of cheap boardinghouses . . . excuse me, ma'am. Perhaps I shouldn't have mentioned those."

Mrs. Dumont pretended not to have heard and did not respond to his apology.

"Oh, we have several entirely respectable inns now, Marshal," said Dumont. "This is a growing city, you know."

Longarm in fact did not think of Fairplay as a city, and although it was night and so impossible for him to get a look at how the place may have expanded, the array of lights laid out before them suggested that it was still only a town and would have to grow considerably more in order for him to think of it as indeed becoming a city.

"The Fairplay will suit me fine, thanks."

"Tim. The Fairplay Hotel, please."

"Yes, sir, Mr. Dumont."

The driver slapped the team into brisk motion, and the distance to the town was covered in short order.

"Tim, go tell Earl the marshal will be arriving. He's to give Marshal Long the Lucky Dog's reserved suite. And Johnny, you can take the marshal's things inside, please."

"You're very kind," said Longarm.

"Not at all. Always willing to help the law, Marshal. Keep that in mind. You can always come to me if you need assistance."

"Thank you, sir." Not that he would need it, Longarm knew. But it was damned nice of the man to make the offer.

He shook Dumont's hand and thanked him again, tipped his Stetson to the man's missus, and ambled into the brightly lit lobby of the tall, narrow Fairplay Hotel.

He could hear laughter from the Silver Dollar Saloon

off to the west side of the lobby, and even out in the lobby the scent of beer and the sounds of gaming tokens ringing on felt-covered tables were a delightful presence.

"Marshal," the desk clerk cried out as if they were long-lost chums. "How nice to see you again."

Longarm was fairly sure he'd never laid eyes on this jasper before tonight, but what the hell. It was always nice to be welcome in a strange town.

He kinda wished he would be able to stay in Fairplay longer, but the work before him would take place far from city lights. Or town ones.

Chapter 4

"I'll see that," Longarm said, "and raise you a dime."

"Call."

"Call."

The fourth man, a gent named Boyd something-or-other, squinted and frowned and finally tossed his cards down. "I'm out."

"Alex?"

The boss of the Lucky Dog needed no time for hesitation. "I'll see your raise, Long, and up a quarter."

Longarm shrugged and folded, as did the other gents at the table. They were playing for small stakes, but Alex Dumont was proving to be a man who didn't like to lose even in small things. Longarm certainly wasn't going to butt heads with him. Especially when all he had was sevens over treys.

"Whose deal?" Alex asked as he raked his winnings into the untidy pile in front of him, all small change. There wasn't a gold coin on the table. But then it wasn't that sort of game.

"Mine," Boyd said. "Let's try a little five-card stud this time. See if I can change my luck here." He picked up the deck and began awkwardly shuffling.

Alex Dumont waved to someone in the back of the

hotel saloon, then motioned. A moment later a lithe and perky little Mexican girl joined them. She was a cute one, with long black hair and pointy little tits that were almost but not quite on display in the deep vee cut of her blouse.

"Pull up a chair, Chiquita."

She did, dragging it in between Dumont's seat and Longarm's. She turned her head and gave Longarm a calculating inspection with eyes that were so hot and sexy it was a wonder there wasn't smoke coming off her head.

"Ma'am." He inclined his head toward her briefly, then returned his attention to the game. Boyd had dealt him a king in the hole and a nine showing. Not exactly an exciting start to the deal. Alex had an ace up.

"Bets, boys?"

"A nickel to see the next one," Alex said, tossing his coin into the middle of the table. The others quickly followed, but no one at this point was interested in raising.

Longarm drew a queen and Dumont a deuce. A fellow named Bernard bet the obligatory nickel to keep the game alive, and they all pitched in.

Alex got his second deuce on that deal. Longarm got a ten. Still not exciting, but he was only one card away from a straight. Across the table Bernard had a pair of kings showing.

"Kings bet a quarter," Bernard said, tossing his money in.

"I'll see that," Alex said quickly.

"Call." Longarm added his quarter to the pot. It was stupid to draw to an inside straight. Everyone knew that. But then if a man was really smart, he wouldn't be playing games of chance anyway. Boyd and . . . Longarm couldn't remember the rather timid fifth man's name . . . the other gent dropped out.

Be damned, Longarm thought. He got his jack to make the straight.

"Kings bet another quarter," Bernard said.

Longarm knew where three of the kings were, so it was

18

unlikely Bernard had anything more than his pair that was showing.

"I'll see that and raise you another quarter," Alex said.

Longarm figured Dumont for two pair. "Call." They went around the table without another raise, and Longarm tipped his king over to show the straight.

"Damn," Alex said. But the man was grinning when he said it. Apparently he liked to win always, but could lose graciously too. He reached over and squeezed Chiquita's thigh. "I thought you'd bring me luck, baby."

"I do bring luck." She laughed heartily. "Jus' not at cards." She turned her head and gave Longarm another of those big-eyed "let's do it" looks.

"Excuse me a minute," Longarm said. "I have to go out back."

"Should we hold the game for you?"

"No, go on and play." He left the table and started toward the back door.

"Not that way," Bernard called out, and pointed toward the lobby.

"Oh, yeah. Thanks." He'd forgotten. The Fairplay Hotel had gone and put one of those modern crapper things indoors. And a urinal trough that was flushed clean constantly with a flow of artesian well water. Classy.

Longarm finished his business there, and came out to find the girl Alex called Chiquita waiting for him at the entrance to the saloon.

"You are one ver' pretty boy, you know that?" she said, taking his hand and running her fingers over his wrist and forearm. She was not what one would call subtle about her message here. "You want to make a little boom-boom tonight, huh?"

"I thought you were with Mr. Dumont tonight."

Chiquita shrugged. "He be here any time. An' he's fat. You know? But you. I bet you got only one fat thing, eh? You wanta stick it in me, babee? I'm sweet, you know. Ver' sweet."

"I'll bet you are, Chiquita, but not tonight." Longarm

19

couldn't understand or condone a man playing around on a dimpled little wife like Alex had. But then he was old-fashioned. He still believed that a man should keep his word. Which was one of the many reasons he hadn't tied himself down in marriage. If ever he did, though, he wouldn't be screwing around on her. It would damn sure be for keeps.

As for Alex Dumont, well, that was his business. It wasn't Longarm's place to judge him.

Longarm shouldered past the Mexican girl, and heard her let out a string of invectives that it was probably just as well he couldn't understand. The word or two that he did recognize gave him the message clearly enough.

Dumont looked up when Longarm returned to the table, then glanced across the room toward where Chiquita was standing there pouting and still muttering.

"You're not interested?" Dumont asked.

"I don't poach in another man's pasture."

Dumont gave Longarm a long looking over. After a few moments he smiled and picked up the deck. "My deal," he said. "The game is plain old five-card draw, gents. Now ante up if you want to play."

Chapter 5

"I hope you enjoyed your stay, Marshal."

"Very much, thanks." Longarm laid his room key onto the counter and waited patiently for the desk clerk to present him with a bill. It would have been a long wait.

"I'm sorry, sir, did you—Oh. I thought you knew. There is no charge, Marshal. The Lucky Dog maintains that suite on a more or less permanent basis. It's all taken care of." The man smiled.

"I didn't expect anything like that."

The clerk smiled some more. "Do you need help with your, um, luggage?" Longarm had dropped his bag and saddle beside the front doors.

"No need for that, thanks."

"In that case, Marshal, thank you for staying with us. I do hope you'll come again."

"You never know."

"Very good, sir. And by the way, your horse is ready. I believe the boy said he tied it on the side street facing the courthouse."

"My horse?"

"Compliments of Mr. Dumont, sir. I believe the animal is from his private string."

Longarm lifted an eyebrow. Then nodded. What the

hell. He'd intended taking a coach the few miles to Alma and hiring a horse there. This would save him the bother. Nice fellow, Alex Dumont. Unless, that is, he had something to hide, some reason to want Longarm in his debt.

"Thanks," Longarm said again, and carried his gear out into the crisp morning air. At this elevation there was no such thing as a warm summer's night, and a man could wake to snow on virtually any day of the year. He'd already known this and had come prepared, having shed his customary tweed coat in favor of a sheepskin-lined leather coat with a high collar and deep pockets.

Private string indeed, he thought when he saw the horse that had been brought for his use. It was a lean and leggy gelding, at least sixteen hands tall and from its lines very likely a pure-blooded Thoroughbred. Its seal-brown coat gleamed with a shine so intense Longarm thought it had been rubbed down with oil. It hadn't been, though. He ran his hands over it just to find out. The shine came from good health and superb conditioning, nothing more. He suspected the handler probably added an ounce or two of corn oil to its grain ration every day.

There wasn't a single white hair anywhere on it that he could see, and it was mannered just fine. Quickly presented each foot when he checked it over, and stood docile and relaxed when he rubbed it all over. The muscle tone beneath that gleaming coat was excellent.

He walked around to the head, lifted the muzzle, and slowly, deliberately exhaled into the horse's nostrils. The horse would know his scent now for as long as it lived.

"You are a fine one now, aren't you, boy?"

The horse flicked its ears, then dropped its head to allow him to rub its poll with his knuckles.

It had the huge, flaring nostrils that allow a horse enough wind for long-distance stamina. The forelegs were set well apart, although the chest was a bit narrow for Longarm's taste. But then this horse was built for speed, not strength. If it ran true to form, it would have no cow sense whatsoever. But then working cattle was not what

Thoroughbreds were meant to do. Their job was to carry a man swiftly over long distances, and he suspected this horse would be very well suited to that task.

Whoever brought it to the hotel hadn't been subtle about how this mount was to be treated. It already carried a headstall with a sweet copper snaffle bit attached. No harshness in handling would be needed here, that gentle bit implied. Which was fine by Longarm. He was no advocate of brutality with animals. For the most part it wasn't the animals that needed rough treatment when things turned difficult. Longarm untied his old army-style headstall and bit from his saddle and tucked them away in his carpetbag. Didn't seem he would be needing them for a while.

He spent a few more minutes feeling of the horse and murmuring softly to it, letting it get to know his touch and his voice. Then he saddled it and tied his carpetbag behind the cantle of his beat-up old McClellan. The ball-buster army saddle was a bitch to ride but easy on a horse.

Time to go find a murderer and earn his pay.

Chapter 6

"Mr. Reed will be with you in a few minutes, Marshal. I've told him you're here."

"Thanks."

The clerk in the silver mine office gathered what looked like some outgoing mail, nodded a polite good-bye, and left Longarm alone in the pleasant but far from fancy outer office.

Longarm was used to waiting. It was part of the job. He crossed his legs, lighted a cheroot, and selected a nearly current copy of the *Police Gazette* from a low table. He was immersed in an article about fly-fishing for trout—the author claimed the key to success was the use of horsehair tippets—when he became aware of another person in the room.

Longarm gave the fellow a surreptitious glance and went back to his trout. The newcomer looked like he'd probably come in to draw his time and skeedaddle down to the city lights where the work would be easier and the comforts more available.

The fellow had no more meat on him than yesterday's ham hock, and looked about half done in even though the day was far from over. He had a scraggly red beard, unkempt reddish-blond hair, and would need a first bath just

25

to get through enough dirt to make a second bathing effective. He sat perched on the forward edge of his chair, eyeing Longarm closely but saying nothing.

Longarm read a little more. And glanced at the red-haired man again. The fellow continued to sit there. Peering. Not bold about it or impolite. But . . . peering at him. It was becoming disconcerting. Longarm folded the paper closed.

"Were you reading this first, friend?" He offered the newspaper to the redhead.

"Oh, no. I just didn't want to interrupt."

Longarm bit back an impulse to grumble that for a man who didn't want to intrude he'd already done a pretty good job of it. "Sure you don't want this? I can read it later."

"Not at all. It's just that I understood you wanted to see me. You, uh, you are Marshal Long? I believe that's the name George mentioned."

George was the Reed Brothers office clerk. And that meant this would be . . . Longarm felt a wee bit foolish, sitting there ignoring the man he'd come to see in favor of somebody else's dead trout.

"Tom Reed," the redhead said with a grin and an extended hand.

"I'm sorry, I didn't . . ."

"Recognize me." Reed laughed. "My brother and I like to get personally involved with our outfit here. One or the other of us is working in the hole at least a part of every shift, night or day."

"I see."

"When you don't have a lot of money to throw at your problems, sometimes it helps to work a little harder."

Judging by the state of the mine owner's clothing, today he might well have been underground personally loading ore carts or tamping powder.

"What can I do for you, Marshal?"

Longarm told him.

"Charlie Ellis," Reed mused aloud after a moment of

26

silence. "Sure, I remember him. He came here, let me see, it would have been in the fall of the year, year before last. Worked here through the winter, until the spring thaw." The grin returned. "Or as close to a thaw as we ever get. It never does get what you'd call warm up here.

"Anyway, about Ellis, he worked topside in the mill. The pay is better underground, but he couldn't stand to be down there. Couldn't stand the cooped-up feeling of it. You see that sometimes. Ellis said it was probably from all those years locked up in prison cells."

"He told you about that?" Longarm was surprised. A man out here could pretty much choose to be who and what he wanted to claim, at least until he did something to trip himself up.

"Oh, yes. He made a point of it, in fact. He told us right off that he'd done time. I don't remember the details, but he was very honest about the whole thing. He said he wanted to make a fresh start and asked us to trust him. Which we did. Dan and I talked it over but there wasn't any doubt in either of us. We liked the man and trusted him and hired him on the spot. We never had reason to regret that either." Reed gave Longarm a look of concern. "I hope he hasn't, um . . ."

"Not that I know of," Longarm said. Which was technically true even if getting there required the splitting of some hairs. Longarm, in fact, did not *know* Ellis was guilty of the robberies and murder.

"That's good, because he was a good worker. And pleasant company too. He always wanted to participate in everything. In some ways he acted like he was still a kid, eager and full of energy and enthusiasm."

That kinda made sense, Longarm thought. Ellis had indeed still been a kid when he was sent off to the penitentiary. He never had gotten a chance to live out the boyhood years.

"Dan and I both tried to talk him out of leaving when he came to us in the spring to draw his back pay."

"Back pay?"

"If a man wants to put some savings by, we let him defer as much of his pay as he likes. We invest it for him at interest—not much, but it helps a little—and the money is available to him whenever he wants. I remember that Ellis signed up for that. In the springtime he came to us and said he wanted to go out and try something of his own. Like I say, we both liked him. We would have been happy to see him stay. For that matter, we'd be pleased to see him return. He would be welcome here anytime."

"He didn't tell you exactly where he was going or what he intended to do, did he?" Longarm asked.

Reed shook his head. "If he did mention anything, Marshal, I don't remember it now. That was a good year ago."

"Of course. Do you recall what the man looks like? I've never met him, and the only descriptions I have are more than twenty years out of date."

"Oh, I remember well enough," Reed said. "But would you like to see his photograph instead?"

"Pardon me?"

"I told you, Ellis liked to participate in everything. He was in the volunteer fire department and the Reed Brothers Marching Moles."

"The, uh . . ."

Tom Reed laughed again. "The Marching Moles. That's the name of our marching band. We work underground, you see, and we're musically blind, so it makes sense in a left-handed sort of way. Anyway, Ellis was active in those functions that I remember for sure. And he might've been on the bowling team too. I have photos of the fire department and the Marching Moles in my office. Come along."

Astounding, Longarm thought. First the good fortune with Alex Dumont. And now actual, recent photographs of his suspect available here.

This assignment was turning out to be a stroll in the park. Hell, if it kept up at this pace, he could expect to run into Charlie Ellis on the trail tomorrow and have the man drop to his knees and begin confessing quick as they came face-to-face.

28

Chapter 7

Longarm had intended to take a ride over the mail route as a means toward putting himself inside the killer's mind, but an opportunity to have a photo of his suspect in hand was just too good to pass up. He made note of the name of the studio that provided the Reed brothers with shots of the Marching Moles, and paid the photographer a visit.

"Of course I still have my negatives," the professor snapped in response to Longarm's request. "Not daft, am I? Hmm?"

Longarm declined to venture an opinion on the subject.

The professor disappeared into the rear of his studio, and returned moments later with a stack of yellowing prints. "This the fellow you mean, is it? Little bald fucker with ears like a bat's wings, eh?"

"How can you tell he's bald?" Longarm asked. "He's wearing a hat."

"Because I remember him, that's why. Besides, I have other pictures of him."

"He posed for you?"

"Didn't say that, did I? But I have one . . . wait a minute." The photographer disappeared again. He was gone longer this time, but when he returned he did indeed have another view of Charles Ellis, this one a scene taken in-

29

side one of Alma's saloons. Ellis was one of four patrons shown relaxing with frothy mugs of beer in their hands.

"Perfect," Longarm said. "I want you to make prints of these for me. I don't need the whole scene, mind. Just give me close-up views of Ellis."

"Why d'you want me to do that?" the photographer asked suspiciously.

"Because I'm willing to pay you for the prints," Longarm told him. He didn't want to unleash a bunch of public speculation about Ellis, and especially did not want to make it broadly known that a United States deputy marshal was looking for him. Ellis could well be still in touch with friends here in Alma, and Longarm did not want to spook his quarry.

"How much?" the photographer demanded.

"You have ... what? Three different views of him? Give me a good print of each one. I'll pay you five dollars." That had to be several times the ordinary rate for a photographic print.

"Ten," the professor countered.

"Don't push your luck," Longarm suggested.

"All right. Five dollars. I'll have them ready for you first thing tomorrow morning."

"You can't make them any quicker than that?"

The photographer gave him a dirty look.

"All right. Tomorrow," Longarm conceded. "First thing in the morning. Now tell me which saloon this scene was taken in."

The photographer squinted at his picture for a moment, then said, "The Pick and Pan. It's about two and a half blocks down."

"Fine." Longarm touched the brim of his Stetson and ambled out into the thin afternoon sunlight. The sun wasn't even down yet and already there was a sharp bite in the mountain air. And this was summer. Winters up here must be a whole lot of fun.

He found a livery where for an exorbitant dollar and a half he could quarter Alex Dumont's brown horse, in-

30

cluding grain rations this evening and again in the morning, then carried his gear to a nearby hotel.

"One dollar," the desk clerk told him, "in advance. You'll have to share the room. You'll share the bed too if we get busy tonight."

"A dollar is fine, but I won't share either the bed or the room."

"I can't make you no promises."

"Sure you can," Longarm said in a tone so mild and gentle that the clerk began to sweat and fidget. Longarm gave the fellow an unblinking stare, and waited patiently until the fellow coughed into his fist and broke the eye contact.

"I expect I could make an exception," the clerk suggested.

"You're very kind. Thank you." Longarm smiled and reached into his pocket for the dollar. "And I'll be wanting a receipt for that, of course."

"Yes, sir. Of course." The clerk handed over a fist-sized skeleton key and said, "All the way to the back on your left."

Longarm wasn't impressed by the key. He knew the type of lock. Anyone with a Barlow pocket knife or a stout willow switch could pick those useless old things in less time than a man with the key could let himself in.

"You might want to be careful who you send down that hallway at night," Longarm said. "I sleep light and sometimes I come awake shooting. You know what I mean?"

"There won't be no trouble, mister."

"Good." Longarm gave him a smile cold enough to put a skim of ice on prickle brine. "I take your word for that."

"Yes, sir. Indeed, sir."

Longarm dropped his things onto the rough blankets that were draped carelessly over the rickety bed, then went back out again. He didn't bother locking the door behind him. There would've been no point.

● ● ●

"Yeah, I remember the fella. Used to come in here two, three times a week. Nice enough fella, I guess you'd say. He'd have a couple beers. Eat a little of that free-lunch spread just like you're doing."

Longarm suspected some of the items, like the fly-specked shards of dried ham, might've been the very ones Ellis ate from more than a year ago. But he didn't say anything. He didn't want to interrupt while the owner of the Pick and Pan Saloon was reminiscing.

"Careful with a dollar. That's one of the things I remember about him. He never played the card games nor paid to screw any of the girls. Tell you the truth, I woulda liked him better if he'd spent more. But he never did. He'd just have his couple beers and leave."

"Yeah, he was a nice enough fella. Always willing to talk. But I never knew him to buy a round for the bar or anything like that. I mean, he wasn't standoffish. Nothing like that. And he smiled a lot. But it's like, I dunno, he didn't say all that much about himself. Come to think of it, I guess he never said anything about himself. He'd talk about work and wages and beer and that was about the end of it. Nothing personal at all." The miner frowned. "I never noticed that before, but it's true now that I think on it. Charlie Ellis never really did talk about anything personal."

"Jailbird."

"What's that?" Longarm asked.

"I said he's a jailbird. Or he was. I don't know where or when but he done time someplace. I'd stake my next pay on that."

"Why do you think that?"

"Couple times I was here standing as close to Charlie as I am to you when Jake Walker, our night deputy, came in to check up on things. It was like Charlie made himself invisible or something. Face flat and eyes empty. No expression. Just . . . waiting to see what the man was gonna

32

do. I've seen that before, mister. Charlie spent some time inside somebody's bars. Count on it. He learned his lesson, though. Charlie won't go back to prison. I could see that about him too."

"You sound like a man with experience."

"I am, mister. Hell, I'll own up to it. I did four years, seven months, and twelve days down in Canon City. Burglary. I don't figure to go back any more than Charlie does."

"You figure Ellis would go under rather than go inside again?" Longarm asked.

The man shook his head. "No, and that isn't what I said. I think Charlie learned his lesson the same as I did. He won't go in again because he won't be dumb enough to do anything again that would put him back inside."

"Care for another beer?"

"No, thank you, mister. Of a sudden I don't feel s' damn thirsty anymore."

"Another time then."

"Yeah. Sure." The fellow tossed off the last of his brew and hurried out into the frigid summer night.

The bartender drifted down to Longarm's end of the scarred and battered planking that served the Pick and Pan as a bar. "I don't know what it is about you, mister, but a couple words from you and people lose interest in drinking."

"Sorry." Not that Longarm meant it. He finished his beer too, and shook his head when the barman reached to refill it. "No, I expect that's enough for me tonight."

"I won't pretend to be sorry," the bartender admitted.

"Good night, mister." Longarm buttoned his sheepskin coat and left the place. No one bothered returning the sentiment.

Chapter 8

The photographic studio was not yet open when Longarm called there in the morning, so he walked over to the post office instead. That was a stop he needed to make anyway.

The postmaster turned out to be a man named Ewald. He was middle-aged, portly, and eager to be of help.

"I didn't really know that fellow from Denver who was killed."

"Barrington," Longarm said.

"That's the name. Forgive me, but I couldn't recall right off. Seems a shame, doesn't it, him dead in the line of duty and me not even remembering what his name was."

"You say you didn't know him?" Longarm asked.

"I met him. That is, he did stop in here and announce himself. But I wouldn't say that I really knew anything about him. He was ... Marshal, it isn't Christian to speak ill of the dead, but that Barrington was an arrogant man. Thought awfully much of himself and had contempt for us stupid yokels up here in the sticks."

"And now he's dead," Longarm suggested, "and if it wouldn't make you feel awful bad, you'd want to think how it serves him right, a snotty, miserable city son of a bitch like that."

Ewald looked startled. "I never . . . I'd never think a thing like that."

"No, sir, of course not," Longarm lied pleasantly. Of course the postmaster thought exactly that. But he'd never in this world be willing to say so, not right out loud he wouldn't. "Actually, sir, if you don't mind, it isn't Postal Inspector Barrington I need to ask you about today; it's the letter carrier Macklin."

"What about him?"

"One of the things I'll need to do is talk with him. Do you know where I can find him?"

"When is more what you need to ask, Marshal. Where you can find him is obvious. Ed spends his time except for Sundays out on the road between here and Leadville. He leaves out of Alma here on Monday mornings. Overnights Mondays at the Widow Shreave's inn on this side of Mosquito Pass. Overnights Tuesdays at the Barton Inn over on the Arkansas drainage side. Wednesdays at the Coz boardinghouse in Leadville. Then it's the reverse of that on the way back. Stops at Barton's on Thursday nights, Shreave's again on Fridays. And he gets back home here Saturday evenings."

"Married man, is he?"

"Yes, he is. Poor fellow's wife can't handle the cold and the elevation up here, though. She tried living here in Alma, but it didn't sit well with her. Had to go back to a lower climate. Nowadays she stays with a sister down in Denver."

"Does Macklin get down to visit her often?"

"Not much time for him to travel that far. He goes down for a few days every few months, I'd say."

"What about his wife? Does she come visit now and then?"

"Not often. Like I said, she can't stand the climate and the thin air up here. Can't hardly breathe up this high, you see."

"What does Macklin do by himself on the weekends

then? And while he's on the trail so much? Does he drink to pass the time? Gamble, maybe?"

Ewald's demeanor changed. His helpful eagerness was fading quickly away. But then the postmaster did not seem a dense or dull man, and probably he could see where Longarm's current train of thought might run. If the letter carrier Ed Macklin were an unhappy man or buried in debt, it might be entirely possible that he himself could be the elusive and so very successful robber who specialized in hitting this mail route and only this one.

"Ed Macklin is a Christian and a gentleman," Ewald snapped. "He spends his Saturday nights writing letters to his missus down in Denver. I happen to know that because first thing every Monday he buys a stamp—pays cash for it out of his own pocket, if you want to know—and posts it for me to send down in the next pouch. Sunday mornings he attends services. Brother Macklin is an elder in the Church of the Upper Room. As I am myself, for that matter." Ewald sniffed. Loudly.

"And both of you gents want me to find whoever it was that murdered Fitz Barrington, I'm sure, even if Barrington was a no-account city fellow."

"Well . . . yes. Of course we do. That is . . . I know I can speak for Brother Macklin as well as for myself about that. Naturally we want the killer brought to justice."

"And I must tell you, sir, that you are being of great assistance toward that end."

Ewald's humor seemed quite fully restored by the compliment. "Yes, uh, it's the least one can do, isn't it."

"Let me see now. This is Friday. That means I can go ahead and take a look at the route. Or get started on that anyway. And tonight I can find Macklin at the . . . what did you say the name of the inn is on this side of the pass?"

"It's run by a widow lady named Shreave," Ewald reminded him. "Agnes Youngblood Shreave. She runs it with her two daughters. Come to think of it, I don't guess I know their names. Neither one of them has ever got mail. And all the widow lady ever receives is her regular checks from the government, one from the war widows' pension board in Mobile, Alabama—that one she gets every month without fail—and the other is from the post office in Denver. She contracts with the Post Office, you see, for the carrier's twice-weekly room and board. Those checks are paid quarterly. You should understand that I'm only telling you these things because of you being a government employee too, you see, and here on official business. I wouldn't say a word if that wa'n't so. Not a single word."

"I believe you, Mr. Ewald," Longarm cheerfully and baldly lied. "I'm sure you are a model of circumspection."

"Yes, well, I am trying to be helpful."

"And the Justice Department is deeply appreciative of your efforts, sir," Longarm said, "which I'll be sure to pass along in the appropriate quarters when I get back down to Denver."

The Regulator clock on the post office wall indicated the photographic studio should be open by now, so Longarm excused himself and went on his way. Helpful fellow, Ewald. And tight-lipped about the private lives of the people he served up here. Of course.

Chapter 9

The photographs were excellent. There were three, enlargements taken from the pictures Longarm had seen in the Reed Brothers offices plus the one candid pose taken in the Pick and Pan, which establishment Longarm now was able to recognize for himself.

To give the man credit where it was due, the photographer had given Longarm full value for his money. All three photos were printed on heavy stock, set into linen mattes, and presented in leatherette folders just large enough to fail to fit into a man's shirt pockets. Longarm stuffed them into a pocket on his sheepskin coat instead, jamming them in beside his gloves, some matches, and several balls of lint.

He collected Alex Dumont's horse and paid for the animal's lodging—it said something when it cost more to stable a horse than a man, but Longarm wasn't entirely sure just what the message was there—and took the smooth and narrow road that led up toward distant Mosquito Pass.

Smooth and narrow it was too. For about three quarters of a mile. After that the track became something of a son of a bitch. And this was in late June. Longarm couldn't help wondering how a man would be able to make it up and over routinely through the snows of January and February the way Ed Macklin had to do twice each week of the year.

There were, he noticed, damned few wagon tracks even though the road had been cut wide enough to accommodate a wagon and team. Big team, though, or mighty light wagon, because as the road climbed it became extremely steep in some stretches, and there were switchbacks where a long hitch would have to be damned well trained, or the wheelers and swing pairs would be stepping in their own traces.

Of course, a really good teamster pushing a really well-trained team could actually get his swing horses to deliberately sidestep over the traces, pull through on a sharp turnaround, and then just as carefully sidestep back the other way to clear the chains and pulling lines without entangling themselves. Longarm had seen it done. On the other hand, he'd seen that little trick attempted somewhat more often than he'd seen it successfully completed. And a long hitch of horses with their feet snared in steel and leather can make for a very panicky and unpleasant situation. No wonder damn few teamsters chose to bring their rigs over Mosquito.

Along about noon Longarm discovered how Mosquito Pass and the Mosquito Range earned their name.

The mosquitoes weren't much for heft. Back home in West Virginia Longarm'd seen skeeters that a man had to fight off with birdshot and big enough to slice and fry once you did.

These Mosquito Range skeeters weren't much more than a pimple on the ass of a West Virginia skeeter. Why, they were tiny bitty little sons of bitches. Longarm almost laughed when the first one came drifting down to light on his wrist, scarcely bigger than a dust mote and thinking it was going to have a drink of fresh blood for lunch. It seemed hardly fair of him to use the thumb of his other hand to squash the wee thing. These Mosquito Range mosquitoes just weren't worth bothering with, he thought with the haughty disdain of a man who knows a proper by-God mosquito when he sees one.

Then some more came along. And some more. And then . . .

The little bastards were nothing for size. But they were hell for mean. And they traveled in packs. Swarms. Huge damned herds of them.

They came at him in black clouds that blotted out the sun and . . . All right. So that was something of an exaggeration. But it was perfectly true that what these little bastards lacked in size they surely made up for in numbers.

They crawled over his cheeks and went to his eyes in search of fluids. They got into his ears. Breathing was difficult because they swarmed around his nose so that he breathed in some of the furry little shits; then when he tried breathing through his mouth, they darted in there too. Nasty-tasting little bastards, mosquitoes are.

Longarm quit trying to swat them individually, and soon realized he would have to adopt other measures instead.

He buttoned his coat to the throat and turned his collar up as if it were the frigid snows of a blizzard he needed to ward off. He put his gloves on. He shook out a bandanna and tied it over his face so only his eyes were exposed. Anyone coming along would likely think he was a robber. Except that anybody else caught out here would be having the same problems and so would likely be dressed the same as Longarm. It would take the threat of a gun to figure out who was and who wasn't a robber with clouds of mosquitoes around like this to torment a man half to distraction.

It wasn't only Longarm that the skeeters deviled either. They attacked the horse with every bit as much gusto as they went after the man. The horse was even less able to chase them away than Longarm was, and had to settle for shaking its head and twitching its ears and becoming irritable as an old maid with her juices flowing.

41

The damned mosquitoes, it seemed, were another good reason why a man might not want to trust himself and his goods to a big hitch over this pass.

It was with considerable joy, then, that Longarm spotted smoke and a cabin roof along about the middle of the afternoon.

The building, which he figured pretty much had to be the inn run by the Widow Shreave and her daughters, was larger than it first appeared. It looked like a rather ordinary cabin had been built in the shelter of a rock overhang, then added onto time after time so now there was a string of small cabins set end-to-end like so many cars in a railroad train, the stationary "train" strung out along the base of the low cliff like a snake hugging a sun-warmed stone.

Smoke came from two of the five chimneys, and there were four horses tied at a hitch rail in front of the middle and presumably oldest cabin.

Longarm unsaddled and put his gear inside a three-walled shed nearby, and turned the horse loose in an open corral along with two others already standing there. A bunker of grass hay insured the animal would have something to eat, and there was a trough of clean water in one corner. A standpipe and runoff, neither in use at this time of year, indicated there would be unfrozen water available even in the cold times.

The place wasn't anything close to being fancy, but it looked like it had been well thought out by whoever put it together.

He hefted his carpetbag and the Winchester in its scabbard and ambled over to arrange accommodations for the night.

And to see if the letter carrier Ed Macklin had arrived yet.

Chapter 10

Agnes Shreave made a sour face and inspected Longarm from top to bottom, looking him over as closely as if he were a melon she was thinking of buying. And an overly ripe melon at that. For a moment he wasn't sure the woman was going to permit him to take a room in her splendid establishment.

"All right," she sniffed eventually. "But you should know I don't allow any drunkenness in my place nor smoking in bed nor making loud noises past ten o'clock when honest folk are tucked in for the night."

"Yes, ma'am," Longarm said meekly. This was a formidable female creature in front of him.

She was probably close to six feet in height and built like a bullwhacker, with massive shoulders and a thick waist and a barrel chest that betrayed no hint of softness. If she had tits, she was able to hide the fact mighty well. Hell, she probably had hair on her chest too, though that was a subject Longarm had no desire to investigate.

Longarm guessed she would tilt the scales at something well over two hundred pounds. And as far as he could see, there wouldn't be a gill of fat included.

Agnes Youngblood Shreave was indeed a very imposing woman.

He figured she was somewhere into her fifties.

"Two dollars a night," she announced, "but that includes hay for your horse. Grain is extra. I feed a hot mix to help the poor animals cope with the cold and the thin air. Little oat, little barley, little bran, lot of corn. It's ten cents a quart. Up to you if you want some."

"I'll take it," Longarm said. "Half gallon now, the same again in the morning."

The widow nodded and turned her head before bellowing, "Betty. Give this gennelmun's hoss a high scoop."

"Yes, Ma." Betty came loping out of what Longarm had taken to be a closet but obviously wasn't. The girl—well, by gender if not by age; she was probably thirty or better—was tall and gawky, with a sharp-edged hatchet face and lanky body. Longarm couldn't tell much more than that for she was bundled deep inside a buffalo coat when she raced off to perform the chore she'd been given.

"Lou," Mrs. Shreave roared. "Take the gennelmun's things to the Scotsman's room."

"Yes, Ma." The second girl darted out of the closet, or whatever the hell the area was at the back of the main cabin. This one was built pretty much like he guessed the first one was, tall and thin with big bones and knobby joints. She had pretty hair, though. Sort of an auburn, he supposed one would call it. Almost red but not exactly.

She gave him a brief, shy look, then dropped her eyes—they were a very pale gray, he saw, large and expressive—and pulled the carpetbag and Winchester away from him.

"Wait," he said. The girl stopped. Longarm turned back to her mother. "You said something about a Scotsman? I don't care to share my room. And you certainly don't look all that busy."

"Too early to tell about busy. But you'll mind I said nothing about sharing the bed. Said it was the Scotsman's room. Which it was. Little while ago, that was. The Scotsman came and stayed with us near a year, lived here and traveled about prospecting for his riches. He favored that

44

room, you see, an' lived in it the whole time. We still call it the Scotsman's room. That's all. And I'm sure you'll like it. Shares the chimney stones with my room, you see. Stays warmer than most, even in winter."

"I see. Thank you."

Mrs. Shreave nodded, and her daughter Lou bolted away into the maze of corridors and tiny doorways that linked the assorted cabins that comprised this high-country way station. Longarm suspected he was going to need a guide when the time came for him to find this Scotsman's room where he would be staying.

"Meals come with the price," Mrs. Shreave told him. "The cooking is plain but I'll fill you right up. If you want something special I might could fix it, but that'd cost you extra."

"I'm sure whatever you serve will be fine," he said, not at all sure about that but willing to find out. The Widow Shreave looked like she would be more comfortable swinging an ax than seasoning a gravy.

"You'll do, honey," she said. He supposed she meant that as some sort of compliment.

He glanced toward the common room, where a handful of men were hunched over a card table. "Has the letter carrier arrived yet?"

"Ed?" She shook her head. "You know Ed, do you, honey?"

"No, but I need to speak with him."

Mrs. Shreave's demeanor changed a little. She became withdrawn and suspicious. "What would you be wanting with Ed now, mister?"

Longarm supposed there was no reason he should try to keep his identity a secret. After all, he would need to ask some questions of Mrs. Shreave too, and might well have to spend considerable time here at her inn if he intended to hunt down Charlie Ellis in the high mountain cuts and valleys. He introduced himself to her and briefly explained his purpose in asking.

"Well, that's all right now. I was scared for a minute,

honey. Thought maybe you was that robber an' killer, though I haven't seen you 'fore now." Longarm noticed that he'd quickly gone from honey to mister and back again as the woman's suspicions came and went.

Longarm pulled Ellis's pictures from his coat pocket and laid them on the narrow plank that served as a desk for the inn. "While we're on the subject," Longarm said, "I'd like to ask if you happen to know this man."

He flipped open the topmost folder. It happened to be the photo taken inside the Pick and Pan.

"Well, I'll be a . . . never mind. Where'd you get this picture, honey?"

"Do you know him?"

"Know him? Of course I know him. That's my friend the Scotsman. Same one whose room you'll stay in tonight."

Chapter 11

"Ellis stayed *here* after he left Alma?" Longarm asked in surprise.

The Widow Shreave scowled and gave him a peculiar look. "Who're you talking about? I thought you were interested in the Scotsman."

"I am," Longarm told her.

"Then what'd you call him that . . . what name was it you said just then?"

"Ellis. Charlie Ellis."

The woman shook her head. "You got that wrong, honey. My Scotsman's name is Charlie, all right, but his last name is Campbell, not Ellis. He's kin to the Highland clansmen over there in Scotland, as I know full well from him telling his stories all those long evenings through. He's a Campbell and proud of it."

He's a liar is what he is, Longarm thought, and apparently good at it. A liar. A thief. A jailbird. And . . . a murderer too? Damn sure could be. But that remained to be seen, didn't it.

"I'd like to know more about your friend the Scotsman," Longarm said aloud.

"Sure, sure. We'll talk. But later. No time right now. I've cooking to do, and baking won't wait. Got to be done

47

when the oven's right or it won't get done at all."

"Yes, ma'am."

"Do you need anything, honey, you ask my Lou. She'll be serving the gentlemen in the common room over there, and your things is all in your room if you need to, um, freshen up or take yourself a nap or anything."

A nap. Right. That'd be the day, Longarm thought. But he said nothing about that notion. The woman obviously meant well. "Thank you, ma'am. I look forward to having that talk with you later."

Not that he could count on learning all that much. If Ellis had spun a web of lies when he'd stayed there—and it surely looked like he had—his talk was apt to have been more fanciful than informative. Anything Longarm learned secondhand via Mrs. Shreave would have to be taken with more than a grain or two of salt for seasoning.

Still, a man sometimes reveals more of himself than he intends when he spends winter nights beside a hot, purring stove.

The woman went off into the labyrinth of tiny rooms, and Longarm ambled down the hall to the saloon—which he'd noticed Mrs. Shreave preferred to call her common room—in search of a drink.

He hadn't seen Lou come back from taking his gear away, but she must have passed by a different route because by the time Longarm got to the bar, Lou was there behind it, and so was her sister Betty, who had shed her coat now to reveal a figure that was identical to that of her sister. Both "girls" were getting a mite long in the tooth to be unmarried, especially in lonesome and woman-hungry country like this where anything in a petticoat could count on as many proposals as she had time to listen to. Both had that gawky, disjointed, slightly awkward appearance that some unusually tall people seem to develop. Both had thin, exceptionally pale skin, freckles by the bucketful, and bad teeth. They were not beautiful. Far from it. But still it seemed a wonder that they would be unmarried and still living with their mother in their . . . he guessed the girls were in their middle to late thirties. Probably infected with some of their mother's man-hating stories, he suspected. You saw that sort of thing now and then. Pity.

He approached Lou—he could tell her from Betty by a smudge of soot on her left cheek; if she washed he might have a time trying to tell one of them from the other—and asked what they had in the way of whiskey. "My taste runs to a good Maryland rye if you've got it."

"No rye, mister. We've got Injun whiskey. Good stuff, though. I make it myself. No snake heads or anything like that. You can pepper it if you like."

Longarm shrugged. What the hell. If grain alcohol mixed with anything that came to hand was what was available . . . "I'll try your concoction, miss." He smiled. "But I'll take the pepper too if you don't mind."

"No offense taken," Lou told him as she brought a crockery jug from beneath the counter and tipped it over a rather small tin cup, pouring only a small amount for him to try.

The whiskey had been colored with something—best not to ask about the ingredients, Longarm knew, because a truthful answer could well destroy the pleasures of the drink—and smelled faintly of . . . he had to think about it for a moment before it came to him . . . licorice. Or horehound. One or the other or, hell, maybe both must have been dissolved in the alcohol.

Lou set a shaker of ground pepper onto the bar, and Longarm tipped a few grains into the cup.

Damned if the girl wasn't right, though. The "whiskey" passed the test. The flakes of pepper descended fluttering to the bottom of the cup easy as you please.

"All right?" Lou asked.

"All right," Longarm assured her.

The girl tipped the jug again and finished filling the tin cup for him.

The pepper was not exactly a scientific means of testing, but it was as good an indicator as a man could hope

49

for. Bad whiskey is generally fairly oily, and pepper grains will float on top of the surface oils. The absence of those oils as indicated by the pepper dropping to the bottom of a glass generally is a good sign.

"To your good health," Longarm said as he raised his glass first to Lou and then toward her sister, who was perched on a stool nearby. He saluted each of the sisters, then tossed the whiskey back.

The flavor was . . . perfectly awful. Damn near took his breath away. But the warmth of the alcohol spread quickly through his belly, and the heat in his stomach would last longer than the taste in his mouth.

He exhaled slowly. Then motioned to Lou for a refill, that first harsh swallow having inoculated his taste buds against the second drink, which should be much more enjoyable.

Lordy, he thought, the things a man has to put up with in the pursuit of his duties. Helluva rough life. You bet.

Chapter 12

Longarm's talk with the letter carrier Ed Macklin was a
disappointment. The man was open enough, even eager
to answer Longarm's questions. The problem was that he
knew absolutely nothing of any obvious value.

Macklin's story was essentially the exact same one
Longarm had already been given by Billy Vail back in
Denver. The postal inspector stayed behind Macklin on
the trail—exactly how far back Macklin didn't know, of
course—and caught up here at the Widow Shreave's inn.
The following morning Macklin left at his usual time.
Barrington was in the common room along with two travelers who were headed east toward Alma. That was the
last Macklin saw of Barrington alive.

No, Longarm reflected after Macklin excused himself
to turn in, there was little in the conversation of any obvious value.

On the other hand, long experience kept Longarm from
counting this as time wasted. In a murder investigation a
man followed every trail he could, and never mind how
important it might seem at the time. You followed all the
leads and kept on doing it until something proved its
worth.

Longarm yawned—Macklin wasn't the only one wanting to turn in at an early hour; there was something about this high elevation and thin air that made sleep seem mighty attractive—and called for a final whiskey before heading to the blankets.

About the only thing new he'd really learned from the postman had—at least on the surface of things—nothing to do with Fitz Barrington or Charlie Ellis. Or Charlie Campbell, as he seemed to be calling himself these days. Rather it was about the mosquitoes. Longarm had assumed there were fewer of the mean and miserable little sons of bitches here because of the smoke streaming out of the inn's chimneys.

Not so, Macklin assured him. The mosquitoes, rattlesnakes too for that matter, inhabited different zones of elevation, lying in layers like a fancy cake, one atop another. But in between those layers would be gaps—slabs of icing between the cake layers, if you like—where the skeeters for some reason did not thrive.

"You can believe it when I tell you, Marshal, that I always look forward to hitting the zones where there's no damn mo'squeeters to devil me and my mule. Surely do. An' after all this time, I know where to expect to find 'em, where I'll lose 'em again. I expect the fella that first put a cabin here knew the same thing. Likely picked this spot so he could sleep free of the miserable damn things. Only makes sense t' do that, don't you see."

Longarm nodded, then idly asked, "The spot where Barrington was killed . . . was that in one of those in-between zones where there aren't any mosquitoes?"

Macklin frowned. "Why . . . I expect it is. Hadn't particularly thought about it before. But now you mention it . . . yes. There wouldn't be any mo'squeeters to speak of right there."

Longarm only grunted and volunteered nothing. But he was thinking that it might have been no coincidence that the killing zone was free of mosquitoes. If a man wanted to lie in ambush along the trail here, he might very well want to choose a spot where he wouldn't be drained of all his own blood before he had a chance to relieve his victim of some.

For a moment Longarm had been tempted to ask Macklin if the robberies also took place in similar mosquitoless spots.

He would've been willing to wager a fair amount of next month's pay that they did.

But he hadn't wanted to mention that to Macklin, who just might pass it innocently along.

After all, the knowledge could become a tool to help him locate the spot where the next holdup was apt to occur.

If, that is, the robber-turned-killer intended keeping on with his campaign. That remained to be seen.

Longarm gazed absently down the hall where Macklin had disappeared, then knocked back his whiskey and set the glass down. "Good night, Lou, Betty."

"Good night, Marshal," they answered as if with one voice.

Longarm turned and ambled off toward his room and a few hours of very welcome sleep.

Chapter 13

Longarm opened three wrong doors before he finally found the one he wanted, identifiable by his gear lying on top of a bench at the foot of the bed and by the huge stone and mortar fireplace on the left-side wall.

Mrs. Shreave had said the room shared a chimney with her own, but she hadn't mentioned that the hearth covered a quarter acre of ground—well, it looked like that much anyway—or that the fireplace arched above that hearth was big enough to accommodate a small ox on a spit if a guest found himself in a mood to throw a party.

A man-tall brass screen was set in front of the fireplace. The floor of the inn, at least in this part of the old structure, was paved with slate, so Longarm figured the screen was there for the purpose of providing privacy rather than protection against flying embers. Otherwise one could see from one room straight through to the adjacent room on the other side. Not that Longarm would've had any inclination to peep at a naked Agnes Shreave. The mere thought of seeing the fat old woman nude, a mountain of pale blubber, was not an appetizing prospect in the least.

He did poke his head behind the brass fireplace screen, however, to ascertain that there indeed was another matching screen in place on the other side. He couldn't see into Mrs. Shreave's quarters, nor she into his. That was fine.

And the fireplace, fueled with chunks of hissing, fast-burning aspen, certainly did keep the room warm. Almost too much so since there was no direct ventilation. If there'd been a window, Longarm would have opened it for the fresh air, and never mind the cold nighttime temperatures at this elevation.

As it was, well, he was sure the room would do just fine.

There was a stout bolt on the door. He slid that closed, then disrobed, draping his clothes on a hat rack placed in one corner and placing his gunbelt and Colt on the floor beside the double-width bed, there being no bedpost to hang the cross-draw rig on as was his usual habit. The bed was large, but built like a cot with neither headboard nor footboard.

It was plenty comfortable, however, as he found to his considerable pleasure when he tried it out. He sighed and stretched out with only a sheet pulled over him, and that more out of habit than necessity as the room was more than warm enough to eliminate the need for blankets.

He would have turned the lamp out, except the one small lamp provided hadn't been lighted, and was in fact not needed, plenty of light from the fire seeping past the brass screen.

Longarm squirmed and wriggled just a bit to get himself comfortable and plumped one of the pair of pillows behind his neck, then let go of consciousness and dropped quickly into a restful sleep.

He came awake with a sharp thrill of alarm, his hand grabbing automatically for the revolver that should have been hanging from the bedpost. Except there was neither a bedpost nor a Colt to grab hold of. He rolled onto his side and fumbled on the floor for his gunbelt.

By the time he found it he realized, if belatedly, that he had no need of a gun right now.

The room was secure. The noise that brought him out of his sleep was that of someone next door fiddling with the fire.

He didn't feel that he'd been asleep very long, but he must have been because the cheerfully snapping fire that had been so brisk and bright a little while ago was almost gone now. Only a dim red glow behind the screen lent any light to the room.

He heard more scraping—it sounded like a shovel blade rubbing on the hearthstone—and even that bit of light disappeared. Longarm guessed whoever was next door, either Mrs. Shreave or one of her daughters, hadn't been in time to rebuild the fire. They would have to start a new one.

Satisfied there was no imminent threat, Longarm returned the Colt to its holster on the floor and tried to go back to sleep.

He heard a series of unidentifiable scrapings and clatterings. With neither windowlight nor firelight now, the room remained in complete and utter darkness. Longarm doubted he would have been able to see his own hand if he laid it on the tip of his nose. He thought about trying that experiment, but was too sleepy to bother. He sighed.

And snapped completely awake.

The bed tilted slightly to the right, on the side toward the fireplace.

Someone . . .

Longarm lurched upright, ready to grapple with the intruder and wrestle the sonuvabitch if that was what . . .

His grasp encountered flesh. Warm flesh. Soft flesh.

"Shhh! Be still." The whisper was so softly spoken he had to strain to make out the words. "Hush now, pretty thing."

The intruder touched him. Ever so gently. Touched his chest. His thigh. Found his cock and fondled it.

Longarm had a moment of panic at the thought that this might be that mound of suet Agnes Shreave perched on the edge of his bed. He reached forward and grabbed—

57

none too gently—for the torso of his unexpected guest.

Whoever she was, it had to be one of the daughters, thank goodness, for the figure he touched was slim.

She recoiled from the harshness of his groping hand, then took it and guided Longarm's touch to her breast, which was small as a tea saucer and hard as a young pear.

"Who . . . ?" he started to ask, only to be rebuked with a repeated, "Shhh!"

He hushed and felt of the girl's tit. She resumed her own tactile search in the blindness of complete dark.

By now Longarm was throbbingly erect, a fact that drew a gasp from the girl who was exploring him. She ran her fingertips very gently up and down the length of his pole; then he felt the bed move again as she shifted position beside him.

She prodded him in the ribs, and Longarm moved aside to let her lie down. Instead of stretching out beside him, however, she bent her lips to him.

He could feel the heat of her breath touch his cock. Then the wet warmth of her tongue. And finally the sweet sensation of his cock being taken into her mouth.

Her tongue was busy and her hands continued to fondle him, one cupping and teasing the heavy sack of his balls while the other roved lightly back and forth on his chest, teasing his nipples and arousing him all the more.

She stayed like that for some time, sucking lightly but holding her head motionless, so that he felt an urgency that became more and more insistent. He wanted her to take him in and out, but she remained still.

Deliberately so, he was sure. Surely she could feel the pounding of his blood in that marble-hard erection. Surely she knew the depth of his need now.

He thrust upward with his hips, driving himself deep into her mouth.

The girl withdrew and chuckled softly in the darkness. "Be still," she whispered. "Let me."

The hand that had been on his chest slid onto his belly and lightly pushed, as if to hold him down.

Longarm wanted almost desperately now to plunge himself deep inside her. But he managed—somehow—to control the impulses and to lie motionless while once again the girl took him into the moist heat of her mouth and poised there, sucking ever so gently, ever so insistently, ever so maddeningly.

Only when Longarm thought he could stand it not one second longer did she finally, mercifully begin to bob her head slowly, slowly up and down, drawing him in and then releasing him. Drawing and releasing. Drawing and . . .

Longarm spewed what seemed a pint of hot cum.

He honestly hadn't felt the rush of the impending release. It came leaping out of him with complete surprise.

And the sensation, so unusually powerful, went on and on for an impossibly long time.

He trembled, but forced himself to remain motionless while the girl finished sucking the juices from him.

He expected her to withdraw and spit, but she did not. She stayed there, holding him inside her mouth, until he was done and then some. He assumed she swallowed his cum—she must have—but he did not ask. He did not want to break this strange spell of raw pleasure.

After a little while she let his cock slip out from between her lips.

By that time Longarm was nearly ready for more. He reached for her, intending to draw her down onto the bed at his side so he could bring her to readiness and return the favor she'd just showed him.

Instead he heard a muted laugh and felt the bed shift as the girl stood up and moved away.

He assumed she would return.

She did not.

He heard a faint scraping as the brass firescreen was moved.

Moments later there was another sequence of scrapes, and soon again there was a soft rose-colored light behind the screen.

Which explained something. The girl had pulled the coals from the dying fire and now was replacing them. Probably stored them in a coal scuttle or a bucket. Something like that.

Now, with the coals back on the stone hearth, she fed kindling onto them. He heard the sighing and dull, leathery *whump-a-whump* of a bellows, and quickly thereafter the newly laid fire burst into bright flame.

Within minutes there was once again a roaring fire that filled the room with heat.

But Longarm much preferred the heat the girl brought into his bed.

He wondered, idly and without passion, which of the daughters it had been who pleasured him so greatly.

Not that it mattered.

He rolled onto his side and slipped back into a much deeper and more relaxed sleep than he'd been enjoying before the, um, interruption.

Chapter 14

Ed Macklin was an early riser. By the time Longarm crawled out of the sack—still in a mild stupor after last night's play let him sleep like a dead man—the letter carrier was already off on the final day of his journey back down to Alma.

Then Monday he would turn around and start it all over again. A man would have to purely enjoy travel to do what Ed Macklin did day in and day out, year in and year out.

"What does he do in the winter?" Longarm asked Mrs. Shreave, who was overseeing the table while the girls did the serving.

"Who?"

"Macklin, I mean. How does he manage to take a mule through the drifts in wintertime?"

"Simple," the fat woman said. "He don't."

Longarm lifted an eyebrow and waited for her to continue.

"Gets too deep up here, he leaves the mule. He can generally get it this far. If it's too bad up above, Ed leaves the mule here at my place—damn gummint pays me board so I'm not complaining, mind you—and he goes on without it. An' before you ask, he has some of those

61

Norwegian snowshoes that he uses so he can go atop the snow and not sink into it."

"Snowshoes are awfully slow," Longarm said, "and they take a man's strength clean out of him."

"These are Norwegian snowshoes," the old woman insisted. "They're long and skinny. Look kind of like flat boards strapped to a man's boot. Uphill they act pretty much like any other snowshoes, but going down they glide over the top of the snow. Darnedest thing you ever did see to watch Ed gliding down the trail slick as an otter sliding on a mud bank. He carries a long pole to steer with and just goes to beat the band.

"You wouldn't think it, but I don't recall Ed ever missing a trip. Well, sort of. Sometimes he can only get one trip in during the week instead of his normal two. But he always makes it across, one way or another. Carries the mail on his own back if the mule can't break through the drifts." She shook her head. "That man is dedicated to his work. You got to say that for him."

"So you do," Longarm agreed.

"Want some more of that porridge?" Mrs. Shreave offered.

"Sure, why not." Yesterday she'd said straight out that she fed cheap but filling. She hadn't lied. Breakfast consisted of milled oats cooked as a porridge and sweetened with honey. There was no milk to pour onto the oatmeal, but then that was hardly surprising considering the near impossibility of getting fresh milk up here and the expense of hauling canned milk.

Longarm would have enjoyed some sausage or bacon or salt-cured ham. But there was nothing of that nature to be seen.

It did not escape his attention that he and the horse were being served what was essentially the same meal. And that the horse got more of it than he did.

Not that he was complaining. No, sir, not a bit of it.

Betty brought the serving bowl around and flopped another generous ladle full of hot porridge into Longarm's dish. He couldn't help eyeing her, trying to see if she would give away any hint as to whether she was the daughter who'd come to his room last night . . . or if it was Lou.

Neither one of them gave the least hint about that, dammit.

Not that it really mattered, he supposed. But a man just naturally had to be curious about which girl it was who was so eager to swallow his load. And then not want anything for herself after.

Still, neither one of them gave any sign that he could detect, and after a while he quit bothering to look. He finished his breakfast and paid Mrs. Shreave for the services rendered, both his own and for the horse.

"Will you be coming back this way again, Marshal?"

"Yes, ma'am, I expect that I will."

"In that case I'll make sure to have the Scotsman's room clean and made ready for you."

"That's mighty fine of you, ma'am. Thank you."

Longarm glanced toward the girls again, but if they heard they did not react, not either one of them.

He touched the brim of his Stetson and headed out to the corral to catch Alex Dumont's fine horse and be on his way. Pleasant as this stop had turned out to be, there were more important things on his mind at the moment than the Widow Shreave's spinster daughters.

Chapter 15

Finding the spot where Fitz Barrington died a harsh and heartless death was easy enough. The reports Longarm was carrying said his body had been found in the middle of the road, smack in the center of Mosquito Pass. Except for the fact that like most mountain passes Mosquito was a rather poorly defined patch of ground, the postal inspector must have met his end right about . . . Longarm peered back and forth a bit . . . right about there.

Not that there were any telltale marks left at this point. Traffic and weather had served to scuff away or cover over the pool of blood that must surely have resulted from two shotgun blasts at close range.

And hell, Longarm might've been fifty or even a hundred yards off in his calculations about the site anyway.

What he wanted here was not so much an exact placement but a look at the sort of spot where the killer must have hidden. You could sometimes learn things about a man if you could come to know his habits and his preferences. This ambush site, Longarm figured, would provide a beginning toward that hoped-for end.

He dismounted and tied his horse, then walked back and forth through the rough and narrow roadway. He could see half a dozen places where a man could easily and comfortably lie in wait, watching the westbound trail first for Macklin and then for Barrington.

Did he deliberately wait for Barrington, knowing the postal inspector was coming? Or was that just his good fortune and Fitz Barrington's bad?

Longarm knew how he could find out. He'd ask the killer. Just as quick as he found the son of a bitch.

Longarm consulted his pocket watch. He'd used up all the morning getting here and poking around. From the pass here he was, as he understood it, about equidistant between Agnes Shreave's inn and the one run by a man named Barton on the Leadville side of the pass. He'd already spoken to the folks at Shreave's, and still needed to talk to Barton.

But he needn't be in any hurry about it.

There was only one road to follow, so if he didn't get where he was going by dark he could just ramble down-hill—on either side—and come to food and lodging soon or late.

For that matter, the notion of staying out in the open for a night or two wasn't exactly foreign to him.

Not yet decided which way to turn next, Longarm walked over to the north side of the road and helped himself to a comfortable seat on a more or less flat slab of rock.

He pulled a cheroot from an inside pocket and, enjoying the pleasure of being between mosquito zones for the time being, carefully trimmed and lighted it.

He was still there, smoking his second cheroot and pondering the lay of the pass and the road climbing up to it from Shreave's—the direction both Macklin and Barrington had come, although not necessarily the route the killer had chosen—when his ruminations were interrupted.

A smear of bright lead appeared on a boulder ten feet to Longarm's right, and a rifle shot sounded from the mountainside high to the south of the pass.

Chapter 16

"Son of a *bitch*!" Longarm was already crouched behind the boulder he'd been sitting on.

He was barely conscious of moving. He'd taken cover almost without thought, and by the time he got behind the boulder he had his Colt in his hand and his Stetson off so it would not serve as a marker for the distant rifleman to shoot at.

Distant. He knew the ambusher had fired from fairly far away. Again this was something that came to him virtually without any conscious thought process.

Deliberately thinking about it now, bringing back to mind everything he'd heard or seen about the time of the gunshot and for those crucial few seconds after, he realized that there'd been . . . something . . . a wink of light perhaps? . . . from high on the south side of the pass. Then the sound of the bullet's impact. And then, a second or more later, the dull, booming report of the shot.

It must've come from . . . there?

Longarm moved a little to his left so he could remain under cover but get a better angle of view toward where he suspected the gunman might be.

For more than a minute he neither saw nor heard anything. Then there was a puff of smoke at the base of a scrub oak about thirty feet to the right of where he'd been looking.

He saw the wisp of smoke. Heard a slug impact the ground some fifteen feet to Longarm's left. Finally heard the rifle shot itself.

Longarm frowned. The first bullet struck a good ten feet to his right. Now this one hit at least that far to his left.

The son of a bitch was warning him off.

This was no assassination attempt. Whoever was up there was deliberately aiming wide. Either that or the bastard was the worst marksman in the history of humankind.

Fuck 'im!

Longarm stood up in plain view and with deliberate care shoved his Colt back into its cross-draw holster so the rifleman could see what he was doing.

No third gunshot followed, further convincing Longarm that he was right about this. That bastard with the rifle didn't want to shoot him. He wanted to scare him away.

Perhaps this was his idea of fair warning.

If so, he was going to be badly disappointed. It would take more than threats to move Custis Long off the trail of a murderer.

Could well be the man believed he was justified in shooting Fitz Barrington—oddly, nearly all killers believed they were right to do what they did—and wanted things to stop where they were.

No chance of that, of course. But it was an interesting possibility. It could even be that the rifleman could somehow be convinced to state his case in the hope that Longarm would let him go free.

Longarm picked his hat up and put it on, then stepped around to the front of the boulder he'd been hiding behind. He waved in the direction of the scrub oak where the rifleman had been hiding. If the man knew what he was doing he would already have moved by now, but wherever he was, Longarm was sure he would be watching.

Longarm waved, then motioned with his arm for the man to come down.

The response was another gunshot. From beneath the same scrub oak, although this time from the other side of it.

Longarm saw the smoke, and for half a heartbeat thought he'd misjudged this situation.

This time, though, the warning shot passed far overhead, scarcely close enough for Longarm to hear the bee-drone sizzle of the slug as it went by. He heard gravel spray as the bullet landed somewhere on the north slope. Finally he heard the third shot.

Right, left, now above. This gent wasn't missing with these shots. No way.

Longarm motioned again for the man to join him. When more than a minute passed without response, Longarm changed the nature of his own signal to the unknown ambusher.

It was a little too far, Longarm thought, for small and subtle gestures to be seen. So instead of the age-old lone digit, he greeted the bastard with a broader stroke.

He held his left hand out and raised his right arm, fist clenched, to smack against his left palm in a classic "fuck you" signal.

Not too damn bright, Longarm decided seconds afterward.

The rifleman's response was a fourth bullet.

This one hit Alex Dumont's fine horse on the side of the animal's handsome head, the slug striking just beneath the ear and drilling into the brain.

The horse collapsed instantly, all four legs folding and dropping the sleek body straight down. It quivered for several seconds and loose, watery dung squirted out of its ass. But the horse was dead and feeling nothing before its belly ever hit the gravel, Longarm was sure.

No, dammit, that bastard up there hadn't missed those other shots. Not if he could shoot like that, he hadn't.

The man's position was probably 175 yards away, perhaps a little more, and it was complicated by being at a fairly sharp downhill angle . . . no, sir, whoever he was, he could shoot a rifle.

Longarm gestured toward the man again, this time with his middle finger extended.

This time there was no response. None at all.

Chapter 17

It was close to dark by the time Longarm crept down to the place where the rifleman had been earlier in the afternoon. He'd spent the hours since then making a wide sweep west, then up onto the craggy slope at the south wall of Mosquito Pass, over the top of that eminence, and stealthily down again.

He was certain that the rifleman would be long gone from his hiding place beneath the scrub oak. But Longarm acted as if he were absolutely dead certain that the bastard was still there.

After all, if you sneak up on an empty patch of ground, the only thing you've lost is some time. And if anyone is around to watch, perhaps a little dignity too.

But if you walk boldly into the muzzle of an ambusher's rifle, you're apt to lose a hell of a lot more than time and dignity.

Longarm made his stalk as carefully as if he could see the hairs growing out of the rifleman's ears.

All he got for his trouble was some lost time. There was no loss of dignity, though, since no one was around to observe this futile operation.

At least he damn sure hoped no one could see, because the only other person likely to be on the mountain was the rifleman. And Longarm would just as soon not have another run-in with him until it was on Longarm's terms.

Once he did hear some horses go by down below, but at the time he was far up the mountainside and screened by some jagged rocks, so he never got a look at who that was.

The rifleman turned out not to have a horse with him, or anyway, Longarm could find no sign of one. Once he was satisfied that the ambusher had slipped away unseen, Longarm spent the remaining daylight examining the ambush point and the surrounding area.

The place where the gunman had lain in wait was very well chosen. From the spot underneath the scrub oak he could see down into the pass itself and, lower and to the right, the road approach from the east or Shreave's Inn side of the pass.

This would have been an ideal place for someone to watch from if, say, you wanted to spot the letter carrier and intercept him in the pass. The first view would have been when Macklin was about a half mile below on the narrow, difficult roadway. That would give a robber ample time to hustle down into the pass and hide himself behind one of the countless boulders there.

It would have been just as good a place to spot someone sneaking along behind Macklin. Postal Inspector Fitz Barrington, for instance.

But Barrington was killed with a shotgun, and the ambusher this afternoon was a very adept rifleman. In Longarm's considerable experience, a gent normally favored one or the other of those two weapons, but seldom both. Nearly anyone might choose to carry a revolver, although some did not. But when it came to long guns, it was generally one or the other, if only because trying to pack one of each would be a real pain in the ass. Besides, a man usually was going to be comfortable and accurate with only the one that he favored, and would likely ignore the other.

Which, Longarm realized, raised the possibility that

there were *two* people involved in the string of robberies and now murder.

It was entirely possible that one acted as lookout, reporting to his partner down below by way of ... oh, maybe hand signals or something on that order ... while the one with the shotgun stayed down in the pass ready to step out and grab the loot.

That would certainly explain how he/they knew Macklin was being followed that day.

The shotgun fancier could have pulled the robbery in the usual fashion, then been alerted by his rifle-carrying buddy that they weren't alone up here.

It made sense, Longarm thought.

Not that it was a certainty.

But it damn sure could've happened that way.

He sat down for a few minutes to have a cheroot; then with what little daylight remained, he tried to find droppings that would indicate the presence of a horse, empty brass cartridge casings that could tell him what rifle this afternoon's gunman favored ... any damn thing that could give him something to chew on.

He came up with ... nothing.

Couldn't find a single damn thing that would tell him anything beyond the few meager facts already in his possession: The rifleman had been right here at this spot; the rifleman wasn't here any longer; the rifleman was a damned good marksman with whatever-the-hell weapon he was carrying.

Hardly enough to get a man all excited about the progress he'd made from a full afternoon of hiking and climbing and sneaking.

Still, if you didn't look you wouldn't see. So Longarm didn't count the time as wasted, merely spent.

He finished his smoke and crushed it out underfoot, then picked his way carefully down into the pass.

When he got there and saw what was waiting for him, he let out a growl and a heartfelt "Aw, shit."

Alex Dumont's dead horse was lying there at the side of the road.

But Longarm's saddle, bridle, Winchester carbine, saddlebags, and blanket were gone.

The only thing remaining was the carcass of the horse.

He still had his coat and gloves, although only because he'd been wearing them. He had his pocketknife, Ingersoll watch, matches, and a handful of cheroots. And he only had those because he'd been wearing the coat with the other things in his pockets when he took off to stalk the rifleman.

Had that son of a bitch seen what was going on and slipped down here to steal Longarm's things?

Longarm wouldn't put it past the cocksucker.

As for himself . . . Longarm just felt stupid.

He hadn't thought. Dammit, he just hadn't thought.

With darkness the temperature was plummeting, and he wouldn't be surprised if it came near to freezing up this high before the night was over.

Not that he had to worry about freezing. A man wasn't going to freeze to death while he was walking. And Longarm damn sure had some walking to do.

He paused first to cut a chunk off the horse's nigh haunch—which was probably the most valuable piece of meat he'd ever tasted—and sear it over a small fire to fuel himself for the hike.

Then, his belly full of warm horse meat, he headed back down toward Shreave's Inn, where he at least could count on being recognized as something other than a deadbeat looking for handouts.

"Son of a *bitch*," he grumbled aloud more than once along the way.

Chapter 18

"Thank God you're all right," the Widow Shreave enthused when Longarm walked into her inn shortly after dawn.

He gave her a sharp look. "How'd you know anything was wrong, ma'am?" He hadn't expected to return here when he left yesterday morning, in fact had mentioned to her that he would be going down to Barton's and probably on to Leadville after that.

She pointed behind the counter and said, "Your things, dearie. When Claude and Adam brought them in last night I recognized them right off. They said that fine horse of yours was dead and your things still on him."

"Claude and . . . ?"

"Adam is his partner. I don't remember the dear boys' last names, but they travel back and forth this way sometimes. I see them prob'ly every few months, I'd say. They took the things off your horse and brought everything here for safekeeping."

Longarm looked behind the counter, and sure enough every bit of the gear he'd thought stolen was piled there. He wasn't entirely sure he appreciated those fellows butting in. But it was good of them to be so thoughtful. He supposed.

"What happened, Marshal?" Betty asked, coming up behind her mother and giving Longarm a look so full of concern that Longarm was pretty well convinced Betty was the daughter who'd slipped into his room the other night. At least until Lou joined her and gave Longarm an equally worried look.

"Are you all right?" Lou asked solicitously.

"Tired. My feet hurt. And I'm mad as hell. But apart from those things," Longarm assured them one and all, "I suppose I'd have to say that I'm all right."

"You didn't tell us what happened to you that your horse would be shot like that," Betty persisted.

Longarm grunted. "Had a run-in with the killer. Or at least I think I did."

"No!" Both girls were wide-eyed. Their mother seemed impressed too.

"Tell us about it," Lou asked.

With a shrug he said, "Not all that much to tell. And I don't know for sure if it was the murderer, but somebody up there didn't want me nosing around the place where Barrington was killed. He tried to warn me off. His last shot killed my horse. Time I got up onto the mountain to where he'd shot from, he was long gone."

"Did you at least get a look at him?" Mrs. Shreave asked. "If you can tell us what he looked like, Marshal, we could prob'ly tell you who you're looking for. We know pret' near everyone in these mountains, one way or another."

"I wish I could tell you," Longarm admitted, "but I never got a look at the man. Just his powder smoke, damn him."

"I'm right sorried to hear you say that," Mrs. Shreave said. "Have you eat your breakfast yet?"

Longarm shook his head. "No, and if you have anything left over, I'd like to have some of it."

"You'll not be having leftovers," Mrs. Shreave declared. "Not after a terrible experience like that. Lou, Betty, honey, you girls be sweethearts for your old mama

76

and go fix up a fine big meal for our marshal here. Betty, go out to the root cellar and bring in some slices off that smoked ham we got from Jeremy. And Lou, you make the biscuits." She looked at Longarm and said, "My Lou makes the finest biscuits you'll ever put a tooth to, Marshal, and you can call me a liar to my face if that isn't the natural truth."

"I'm sure you're right, ma'am."

"Now I want you to know, Marshal, that we don't keep any horses. Too expensive to feed them, you understand. If we need to go anywhere we'll just catch a ride with one of the gentlemen passing through."

"Uh-huh."

"Before this day is over there's bound to be someone coming by that you can travel down with so's you can get another horse."

There was no chance he would ever find another horse as good as the one that son of a bitch murderer killed, but Mrs. Shreave was right that he would be needing a new mount.

On the other hand, there were still some things that needed doing up there. And he could do them best if he were not encumbered by a saddle horse.

"I don't suppose," he said, "you could send for a spare horse instead of me having to go down after one."

"I suppose I could do that. But why?"

His smile held no mirth in it. "Because I intend to go do me some hunting while I'm up here, ma'am."

"Two-legged game, Marshal?"

"The very same, ma'am."

She nodded as if that were the most natural thing she could think of. "Tell me whatever it is you want to carry with you, Marshal, and I'll be glad to provision you free of charge. It will be a blessing to us all if you can find the monster that murdered poor Mr. Barrington and keeps a-robbing dear Edward."

"Thank you, ma'am. You're very kind."

She sniffed. "Not a bit of it. A mother with two daughters as lovely as mine has to fret when there's a fiend on the loose, you know."

"Yes, ma'am, I'm sure that's true."

"Just you go on now, Marshal. Into the common room there and have yourself a seat. My babies will have your breakfast ready in no time. Then I want you to tell me every little thing I can do to help you.

"I don't have all that much, Marshal, but if it will help protect my girls, you're welcome to anything or everything under this roof."

"Thank you, ma'am. Thank you very much."

Chapter 19

Longarm figured he was about as prepared as he could be, everything considered. He had his Winchester—thank goodness for honest travelers like Claude and Adam; if he ever had the chance Longarm damn sure wanted to buy those gents a drink or three—and a pack of cold food that didn't need cooking. Smoked ham and sausages, biscuits baked hard and wrapped in muslin, some raisins and dried apples, a little of this and a bit of that. The important thing was to get along without building a fire.

He figured he'd be able to find water to drink. There was still snow, old and icy, in the shadowed hollows. And he tucked a bottle of rye whiskey into his pack too to help keep the chill at bay overnight.

Chill? It was going to be a natural sonuvabitch for cold up there above the pass, so he carried a sleeping sack that Lou and Betty sewed together for him from three heavy blankets folded in half and nested one inside the other so the resulting pouch was closed snug and windproof on three sides, and open only at the one end so Longarm could crawl inside and poke his head out the top. A bag like that was as good for sitting in as sleeping in, and he figured to get plenty of use from it once he got onto the mountain.

What he was doing, of course, was going hunting. But more with his eyes than his rifle. He would shoot if he had to, but he wanted to get more satisfaction from that gunman than a simple bullet could provide.

He wanted to find the bastard and see if he worked alone up there or in company with a partner—it would just naturally hurt Longarm's feelings to pull a sneak on the man with the rifle, only to be caught unsuspecting by another one with a shotgun—and learn what he was about.

Most of all, Longarm wanted to ask the fellow some questions. Lots of them.

So he hiked warily up the road toward Mosquito Pass, leaving the public road a good mile and a half below the notch where the road cut through from the Platter River drainage over to the Arkansas River side.

From there he continued climbing, but as stealthily as if he were stalking elk.

In fact he was after game that was much more deadly than anything nature put into these mountains, and almost as wary.

Longarm's butt hurt. He'd finally managed to find a decent lookout point that was reasonably free of mosquitoes, but it meant making his cold camp on a slab of rock.

And no matter how often you shifted positions, sitting or lying on stone became almighty painful after a spell. In Longarm's case that "spell" had lasted into the fourth day now, and all he'd received for his trouble was aching muscles and a nagging cough.

He had no idea what the temperatures were getting down to overnight at this elevation, and it was probably just as well that he did not. If he knew how bad it was, he'd probably be tempted to give up and look for a more comfortable place to do his watching.

Funny thing about that, though. A compromise here and another tiny one there, and pretty soon there was no point in bothering because by then you'd traded away your chances to succeed in exchange for a bit of comfort.

This perch where Longarm sat now was on a ledge of granite just at timberline. A pair of runty, wind-twisted cedars that looked old enough to be kin to the original cedars of Lebanon managed to eke out a living with their roots in a crack in the rock behind him. Their limbs weren't shit for a windbreak, but he figured the outline of their ragged shape would insure he couldn't be silhouetted against the sky from down below and they would help keep him from being spotted up here.

His view stretched off toward the north and to the west for more miles than Longarm could count. Below and before him the mountain ranges jutted in raw, rugged spines like waves on a gigantic ocean of stone and earth. In the distance he could see more than a score of peaks that were still mantled in white, and closer in the lesser ranges were black with thickly forested slopes.

He could see a little of the Mosquito Pass road. A stretch of no more than a hundred yards or so was visible to him. The pass itself was below his line of vision.

Instead, however, he had a clear and complete look across the hillside where the rifleman had lain in wait.

And he had a backdoor view of most—certainly not all, but most—of the likely routes a man on foot might choose to reach that slope.

The rifleman's game was silent watching.

Longarm figured to beat him at that game. And any other the bastard wanted to play.

If, that is, the man ever came back.

Longarm hadn't bothered trying to figure out just exactly how long he was prepared to sit here in this miserable damned aerie waiting for the man to return.

But whatever his give-up point, he hadn't reached it yet. He still had a little food, and more to the point, he still had a full complement of determination. After this much time he might've considered swapping one of his balls—just one, though, thank you—for a cheroot and a warm place to smoke it. But he wouldn't give up a chance at that rifleman for all the comforts in the world.

Nossir, he expected he could be just about as stubborn as anybody when the need for that arose. And right now seemed a pretty good time to prove that.

Chapter 20

It was a damn good thing Longarm wasn't chewing a cud of tobacco. He was so startled he likely would've swallowed it if he did have a chaw.

The rifleman stood up. Just . . . stood right up in plain sight, there at practically the exact same spot where he'd been when he shot Dumont's horse down.

The thing was, this was the afternoon of the fifth day since Longarm found this perch, *and he'd never seen the gunman come to his spot.*

Surely the bastard hadn't been sitting there this whole time.

No. Couldn't be. A man had to move around some. If nothing else, he had to go take a leak from time to time. There'd no man been born who'd been immune from that requirement.

And Longarm knew good and well the fellow couldn't have done any significant moving around without being spotted from up here.

No, either he'd slipped in before daybreak—and that was certainly possible—or he was so almighty good at sneaking about in the woods that he'd taken up his place without Longarm seeing him come.

Early morning, Longarm decided. *Had* to be.

Even so, this bastard had earned a measure of Longarm's respect. He was plenty good if he'd sat there the whole day through without Longarm seeing him.

Longarm found himself wishing for a spyglass so he could get a better look at this patient and entirely too accurate rifleman. The distance was a good quarter mile, and Longarm couldn't make out any detail of what the fellow looked like. Certainly wouldn't have been able to spot him in a crowd if they came face-to-face somewhere.

The man was dressed in a buffalo coat—the dark, drab fur probably helped him blend into his surroundings underneath that scrub oak—and either had a helluva head of hair on him or was wearing a fur cap of some kind. It was too far for Longarm to decide which, although he'd've wagered on the hat.

The man was, of course, carrying a rifle, obviously a full-sized rifle and not some saddle carbine, but again Longarm was too far away to make out any details.

The man stood. Stretched. Stamped his feet a few times. Likely they'd gone to sleep on him. That happened to Longarm too if he didn't make it a point to flex and move them around some every time he felt them start to lose feeling.

Once he was done getting his blood to circulating again, the man gave one last glance over his shoulder in the direction of the road, then craned his neck and peered from one horizon on around to the other.

When he did that, his eyes naturally swept right at Longarm and then moved on. Longarm would have to admit to having something of a spooky feeling when the rifleman seemed to be peering straight at him. But the man couldn't see anything up here, not with Longarm sitting stone still and his silhouette broken up by the cedars behind him. Longarm was positive about that. Almost positive. He worried just a wee bit. Then the rifleman reached down to scratch himself, unbuttoned his fly, and took what surely had to be the longest piss Longarm ever knew of. Fella sure could hold his water, by damn.

When all that was done, the man laid his rifle in the crook of his elbow and set off around the side of the mountain toward the south.

Longarm watched him out of sight; then he too stood and did the stretching and stomping and piss-taking.

It seemed he had some more walking to do.

Chapter 21

"Son of a *bitch* but it's cold up there."

Longarm dropped his things onto the floor of Mrs. Shreave's common room. He didn't even pretend to be tidy about it. He opened his coat, shucked out of it, and dropped it on top of everything else. The whole thing made a powerfully smelly heap, which he noticed now that he was in where there was a fire and folks.

Funny, but he honestly hadn't been conscious of his stink up there on the mountain.

"I need a bath," he said. "And food. And some clean clothes."

Lou paused in the act of picking up after Longarm's mess. She wrinkled her nose and sniffed, then loudly agreed. "I'm glad you said something about a bath. The rest of us will all appreciate that." She was, fortunately, smiling when she said it, though.

"Let me have a drink first, please."

Betty poured him a generous knock of the vile, blessed bar whiskey. Longarm tossed that back and generously allowed her to pour him another.

"Lou's getting your bathwater now. We'll bring the tub into your room, Marshal."

"Thanks."

"D'you want to wait for us to cook something for you? We have some leftover stew on the stove. It should still be warm."

"I'll take the stew now, thanks, and something more later."

He'd been out for eleven days, the last three of them without anything in his belly but snowmelt water. And damn-all little for the two days before the food ran completely out.

Every day, though, he'd managed to follow the rifleman a little closer to the son of a bitch's lair, wherever it was he went at night.

The man didn't always go out to watch the road, but Longarm had been able to follow him far enough the second time he saw him that he was able to pick the man up again each day and then, each evening, follow him just a little way closer before losing him in the sudden mountain darkness that fell with scarcely any twilight to soften the blow.

Longarm was getting close. He felt it. And he hated having to come down to reprovision. Had to be done, though. He simply had no choice about it. Not if he wanted to have stamina enough to do anything once he found the rifleman's nesting place.

He just flat needed some warmth and some food. And one good night's sleep in a real bed.

Then he'd be ready to tackle grizzlies if that's what it took. Not that he'd seen any grizzlies in this particular range. There were a hell of a lot of black bears up there, and some goats wandering about up above timberline. But no grizzlies. Thank goodness. Those fuckers were downright mean and not to be trusted.

The most dangerous game of all, though, was the quarry Longarm was tracking. Or anyway would get back to tracking tomorrow.

That, however, was tomorrow. This was today. And, oh, that bath was gonna feel fine.

• • •

Longarm was neck deep in soapy water, warm for the first time in what seemed ages, and about as happy as a dead pig in the sunshine. He had a cheroot between his teeth, a lilac smell in his nostrils from the soap the girls gave him, and a fire in his belly from the glass of whiskey sitting on the seat of a chair next to the copper tub where he was soaking, and from the three bowls of stew he'd wolfed down before retiring to his room and the bath.

This was good.

He did have something of a start when the doorknob rattled. Someone was trying to get in. Well, the hell with them. Whoever it was could just wait until he was done with his bath. He'd been thinking about this—and other things—for days now and he wasn't going to cut any of the pleasure short.

"Marshal? Are you in there?" It was a male voice. Reason enough to not bother unbolting the door. Longarm thought he recognized it as Ed Macklin.

The postman could just wait, dammit. He'd be here until morning.

Longarm reached for his glass and had another satisfying swallow. Lousy though it was, the whiskey was commencing to taste good to him. That was probably a bad sign—of something—but the hell with that too. The way he figured it, he'd earned a few minutes of relaxation while he was up on that mountain hunting the rifleman. And he did surely intend to relax now that he was . . .

He froze in place, the whiskey forgotten in his left hand while his right sought the much-worn grips of the big Colt that he'd also placed on the chair seat. What he was hearing now wasn't Ed Macklin at the door. It was . . .

He relaxed and smiled. Big.

What he was hearing was someone over there scraping coals on the hearth. Or more likely, he figured, shoveling coals *off* the hearth. There was a lamp burning in the room, so this time it looked like he was going to get a look at his visitor.

89

Grinning, he set the whiskey aside and waited for the brass screen to be pulled aside.

Even expecting the visit as he did this time, he nonetheless was surprised by what he saw peeping out from that fireplace opening.

It wasn't Betty or Lou over there.

It was Betty *and* Lou.

And both of them were already shedding their dresses even as they stepped into Longarm's bedroom.

Chapter 22

"Come on now. Fess up. Which one of you was it visited me the last time I was here?"

The girls looked at each other across the hairy plateau of Longarm's chest and giggled.

Neither, he noticed, offered to answer the question.

My, oh, my, but they were a pair. Without clothes their coltish awkwardness disappeared and they were as sleek as otters, as slim as willow withes.

They'd unpinned their hair and dropped their clothes, and if either one of them had the tiniest lick of modesty she'd sure left it someplace else.

They came prancing across the room and knelt beside the tub, one on either side of him. First Lou kissed him. Then Betty did. Then Lou reached for the dish of soap while Betty fished around in the water for the washrag— the rag wasn't the only thing she found while she was feeling around down there—and the two of them set about scrubbing and rubbing and cleaning him like he wasn't yet out of diapers.

There wasn't a square inch of him that they missed. Hell, Betty even spread the cheeks of his ass wide so Lou could get in there with the soap and the washcloth and scrub that too.

They washed his pecker so clean he was afraid they were going to finish off the job by boiling it just to make sure.

Then they helped him out of the tub and, each of them with a towel made out of old flour sacks, rubbed him dry until his skin likely took on a polished sheen.

Once he was about as thoroughly clean as mortal man could ever get and dried to a fare-thee-well, they took him by his hands and led him over to the big bed.

It didn't take a whole lot of persuading to get him there, he would have to admit.

They laid him down and, again one on each side, stretched out beside him with their heads at the wrong end of the bed.

Longarm couldn't quite figure out what these girls were up to. He found out quickly enough.

What they had in mind was to give him another bath.

With their tongues.

Lordy, but the sensations the two girls gave him were almost more than he could bear.

They licked the soles of his feet and sucked his toes and ran their tongues into the hollows between his toes, not missing a damn thing.

They lingered for a spell on the insides of his knees, then wiggled and licked their way higher, turning him onto his belly once they got thigh high.

Longarm couldn't believe what they were doing. But at least now the completeness of that bath began to make sense.

Damned if one of them—he couldn't see which—didn't slide her tongue into the crack of his ass and go to licking and sucking him there too.

That was . . . extraordinary. To say the least.

Then they rolled him over and started the process over again, this time moving from his head downward.

This right here, he figured, was probably about as close to heaven as he could ever expect to get. But, oh, my. This *had* to be almighty close. Just had to be.

By the time Longarm got around to asking his question, he'd satisfied Betty three times and Lou twice—Lou was a tiny bit slower to pop than Betty was—and felt about as wrung out as that washrag they'd used on him earlier.

Not that he regretted getting that way. Not hardly.

He sighed and gently stroked the back of Lou's head while Betty explored inside his mouth with her tongue.

"D'you really want t' know, honey?" Betty asked.

Longarm thought about that for a few seconds and then, grinning, shook his head.

"Good," Lou said.

"Because we wasn't gonna tell you anyway."

The two burst into a fresh round of giggles and then bounced to their feet in perfect synchronization, even though he would've sworn neither one of them made any kind of signal to the other. It was spooky, really, as if the two of them thought with one brain.

Not that Longarm was criticizing them. Nossir, he was not.

Each of them swiftly bent to plant a chaste kiss onto his forehead, and then, again moving as if they were a single person, they ran lightly across the room to disappear behind the fire screen.

"Damn!" Longarm whispered into the silence they left behind.

Chapter 23

"Well, I'll be a son of a bitch," Longarm marveled. "The fucker lives in a cave."

And so he did. For the past three days Longarm had been following the rifleman by watching for him in the mornings, picking him up from the place where he'd been previously spotted the evening before, and then backtracking him once the man was safely on his way.

This final morning Longarm was able to finish the job by tracking with his nose. The rifleman was much too savvy to leave a fire burning, and there was no smoke to see by the time there was a blush of light visible on the eastern horizon. But the man hadn't been able to keep the just-killed fire from smelling like a just-killed fire, and once Longarm got close enough to get a whiff of that distinctly smoky odor, it was simply a matter of walking upwind until he found the source of the scent.

Which turned out to be a cave opening in the mountainside with no visible hints to indicate any human being had ever passed this way.

No attempt had been made to hide it. Which in itself was one helluva fine way to hide it. In plain sight, with nothing whatsoever to call attention to this particular dark and gaping opening in the rock of the mountain.

Longarm practically admired the son of a bitch. Likely would have if the fella wasn't a murderer.

As it was, though, he could reserve no sympathy for this man. Fitz Barrington hadn't gotten any.

And who knows what could happen next if this were allowed to go on.

At least Longarm was going to bring this problem to its conclusion in time to avoid another robbery . . . or worse. That was what Ed Macklin had wanted to talk about down at Shreave's that evening.

When Longarm finally got around to getting dressed after his, um, bath, he'd found the letter carrier in the common room having a cup of coffee. Next week's delivery would be Macklin's first round trip of the month. That was the delivery the robber always chose to hit. The first carry only. Never any other. And always on the Fairplay-to-Leadville leg of the trip, never on the back-haul.

Macklin fully expected to be robbed, and now he was afraid of being murdered too. The killer would surely know he was the subject of a redoubled investigation now that Barrington was dead. Macklin was afraid the man might be jumpy enough to start pulling triggers with no more provocation than the noise of a rock falling or a squirrel chittering.

Ed Macklin did not want to end up lying in the road with his brains littering the gravel.

Longarm didn't blame him.

But now, with the hideout discovered, things were looking up in that regard.

Right now it was—Longarm craned his neck and peered overhead rather than bother digging his watch out—about an hour and a half short of straight-up noon. The rifleman wouldn't be back here until well after dark. From the place where Longarm had always lost him in the night shadows, it would be a good forty-five-minute walk. So allowing for slower going walking at night,

Longarm figured he wouldn't be back here to his hideout for roughly an hour after good dark.

Longarm could wait for him along the trail and take the man down on his way home.

Or he could do this the easy way.

He would, he decided, do this the easy way.

The rifleman came into his cave with all the certainty of a man moving about in his own bedroom—which, in a manner of speaking, he was—and paused about ten feet in from the mouth where he'd constructed a circular stone fire pit. Placed where it was, the pit was far enough inside to let the smoke dissipate some before it lifted from the mouth of the cave, and because of a peaked ceiling rising toward the entrance, it seemed likely the smoke would naturally rise toward the cave opening rather than filling the interior.

A dark, ages-old varnish left behind by the smoke from countless fires showed this fellow was not the first who'd taken up residence here.

But this was the one who lived here now, and this was the one who held Longarm's interest. Let the scholars worry about the peoples of the past if they wanted to.

Once the rifleman was inside, Longarm could hear him just fine, even though a cloudy, moonless night kept any light from entering the naturally formed but man-enhanced interior.

He heard a clink of metal against stone, and figured that would be the man setting his rifle aside. Good. But then he was in his own nesting place, wasn't he, and had no need to be wary any longer.

Longarm heard some unidentifiable thumps and something that might have been a sigh. The man sounded tired. But then he'd been out since dawn. Must not have spent today laid up watching the road if he was so worn out now.

There was a scrape of leather boot soles on the gritty rock floor, then a hint of glowing red as the rifleman raked the ashes in his fire pit to expose a few live coals.

Longarm heard the crackle of kindling being broken, and soon after saw a new flame leap bright and yellow into life.

Longarm could see the rifleman clearly now as he patiently, carefully fed splinters of pine fatwood onto the fire, then wrist-thick wands of aspen, and finally some chunks of mixed aspen and pine, until he had a fine, roaring blaze that filled the cave with heat. And with light.

When the man turned to come back into his living quarters he found himself looking into the muzzle of Deputy Custis Long's .44 Colt as Longarm sat comfortable as a tick on a hound's ass in the fellow's own handmade rocking chair.

"Welcome home," Longarm told him calmly.

Chapter 24

The man glanced toward the rifle that was leaning against the cave wall about eight or ten feet from where he now stood.

"Go ahead if you want to," Longarm told him. "I've always figured a man's got a right to die if that's what he really wants."

"You'd . . . you'd shoot me, wouldn't you?" the fellow asked.

"Hell, yes, I'd shoot you. You shot at me, didn't you?" In fact the man had not and Longarm knew it.

"I never," the man blurted out.

"Yes, you did. Down in the pass. And at that I was lucky. At least you didn't gun me down with a shotgun like you did Fitz Barrington."

"Barrington? He the man that mail robber killed?"

"That's right. That's the name of the postal inspector you shot and killed after your last mail robbery."

The fellow looked quite seriously offended. "Not me, mister. I wouldn't have a damn shotgun. A rifle, that's my pleasure, not some scatter-to-hell short-range piece of shit like a shotgun. Anyway, what do you care who killed that . . . whatever his name is. I mean was. Whatever his name was. Or are you jealous because somebody got to the mail before you could steal it? Well, go ahead. Rob me if you want. You can have it all. Everything I've found. It's all over there in that trunk."

The man pointed. Longarm did not look behind him. Yes, there was a trunk there. Longarm was sitting not three feet in front of it. So what. The man wasn't going to give himself a distraction that easy.

"Sorry t' disappoint you, bub, but I came up here to arrest you, not rob you." Longarm pulled his wallet out and flipped it open to display the badge he carried pinned inside. "I'm a United States deputy marshal, mister, and you are under arrest."

"Arrest? What the hell for? I haven't done nothing." The man squinted, then groaned. "Aw, shit. You're the one in the pass a couple weeks back, right? Now that I think on it, I recall that hat an' coat. I shot your horse, right?"

"Uh-huh." Technically speaking, of course, he'd shot Alex Dumont's horse. It didn't seem a point worth quibbling over at the moment.

"You were looking for me. Or you were looking for my gold. And that's just as bad. Only right that I'd stop you from being up here. You damn flatlanders got no right up here. The gold on this mountain is mine. You were looking for it. That's why I shot your horse. I was within my rights. Just protecting my property. Man has a right to protect what's his. Everybody knows that."

"That's a public road down there, and I was minding my own business when you threw those shots."

"Yeah, well, it didn't look like that to me, I'll tell you. And I never shot at you. Just the horse. If I'd wanted to shoot you I could've. Could've put a ball through your brisket any time I was of a mind to."

Longarm glanced past him to the rifle. The thing wasn't much to look at. Just an old Sharps, and not even a modern one at that. This one had the old-fashioned breachloading loose-powder-and-ball action that had been around since sometime before the recent War Between the

States. Damn thing had a big old musket-sized nipple on it and a stock so battered it looked like it had been through three wars, not just one. Longarm had seen plenty of these old-time Sharps before, but always carbines. This one had an octagon-shaped barrel that was full rifle length. He guessed it to be twenty-eight inches, give or take a bit. The carbine barrel was round and not but maybe sixteen or eighteen inches long. He didn't think he'd ever seen one quite like this.

It was a natural fact that this fellow could shoot the ears off a fly with it, though, old and nasty-looking or not.

"How'd you come by that rifle?" he asked.

The man's chest puffed out some. "You ever hear the term Sharpshooter?"

"Course I have," Longarm told him.

"Well, me and some of my friends was the originals. General Grant, he had the best rifle shots in the whole damn army collected together, and we shot targets against one another until there wasn't but two squads of us left. Once it was down to the best of the best, we was given those special-made Sharps rifles and told to go kill us a bunch of rebels. And if you're a Johnny Reb yourself, Marshal, then fuck you because I killed a heap o' your kin till the war ended all the fun we was having."

"Fun, was it?"

"Damn right it was," the Sharpshooter snapped. But there was something in his eyes that belied that brag. A hunted, haunted look that made Longarm think it wasn't the lure of gold that brought him up to this isolated cave so far from warmth and people.

Longarm decided that was a notion best not pursued. This poor son of a bitch had troubles enough without Longarm coming along and picking at his unhealed scabs all these years later.

"Why should I believe you about any of this?" Longarm asked.

The Sharpshooter thought about the question for a

while. Then shrugged. "Damn if I can think of any reason you should believe me."

"Funny thing is," Longarm said, "I do."

"Why?"

"Mostly, I suppose, because you could've shot me in the pass that day if you wanted. I knew that at the time. If you'd wanted me dead I would be. You wanted to scare me off. You picked one dumb-ass way to try and do it. In fact, you did just the opposite. But I can see how you might've thought about it at the time."

"You don't want my gold then?"

"I don't want your gold, mister. What I want is the man that murdered Fitz Barrington."

"I can't help you there, mister. Marshal, I mean. That is, I seen the fella, oh, twice, I think. When he was waiting for the mailman to come along."

"You *saw* him?"

"Sure. He don't know that. But I seen him, all right. I was laying up there like I do, waiting to see was anybody sneaking around after my gold. This robber, I wondered about him the first time I seen him. Then when I found out it was just the mail he wanted and not my gold, I left him alone. I mean, it isn't my mail to watch over, is it?"

Longarm didn't bother to answer. After all, the Sharpshooter was right. He wasn't obligated to defend the United States mail.

"Did you get a good look at him?" Longarm asked.

The Sharpshooter shrugged and said, "About as good a look as I got of you. It's a pretty good way down there, and I wasn't paying much attention. Not once I knew he didn't want my gold."

"What can you tell me about him?"

"Now I never got a good look at his face, mind, but I seen he was wearing a buffalo-hide coat like the army issues these days. And a black slouch hat. Might be an old Kossuth, though I wouldn't know that for sure, of course. Kinda a droopy thing anyway. And he's a mite plump."

102

"Plump?"

"Yeah, I'm pretty sure he's plump. I mean, anybody'd look thick with a buffalo coat on. But this fella . . . he walks plump. Not fat exactly. He don't waddle side-to-side. But he walks . . . different. Plump."

Longarm understood that. Sort of. "Were you watching when he shot Barrington?"

"Am I gonna get in trouble if I tell you?"

"No, you won't be in any trouble for not reporting it or doing anything about it if that's what you mean."

"Well, then, yeah, I guess I did see that too. He held up the mailman and the mailman dropped his pouch and the fella motioned for the mailman to go along. Which he did. The mailman, I mean. Then . . . it's not how you might expect a fella to act after he's pulled his job . . . but instead of stepping out into the road to collect his loot and sneak off with it, he slipped back into his hiding place. On this side of the pass, that was. I'd seen him go in there, mind, and I'd seen him come out, but when he was hiding there he was below my line of sight, so I couldn't be sure what-all he was about while he was waiting there. But anyway, he slipped back out of sight there and waited some more.

"Pretty soon I could see why. This other fella came sneaking along. Must've thought he was pretty crafty, jumping from rock to bush to boulder and coming along quick but foxy. You know?"

Longarm grunted. He didn't want to distract the Sharpshooter. Not right now he didn't.

"That robber, he let the mail pouch lay out there in the road like it was bait or something. And sure enough, the fella that was following along behind the mailman, he got up into the pass and he seen the mail pouch laying there and he just naturally went over and picked it up.

"That's when the fella with the shotgun came back out to where I could see him. Had this . . . Barrington, is it?"

Longarm nodded.

"Right. Well, he had Barrington cold. Had that shotgun

103

leveled at him from close up. Then Barrington said something—I couldn't hear what, you understand, since I was way the hell up on the hillside there—and the fella with the shotgun acted . . . I dunno. Scared, I'd almost say. I mean, he was the one with the shotgun in his hands, but it was him that was acting scared. You know how I mean, the way a man's shoulders will hunch and he'll sort of pull into himself like as if he's expecting to be hit or something."

Longarm nodded again.

"I couldn't hear, but I could sure see that much. Then Barrington, he said something else and he shook the mail pouch. Which he was still holding. He shook it at the robber like you'd take and shake a cookie under a kid's nose if the little son of a bitch has been caught taking what he's not supposed to. Barrington acted like he was dressing down the fella with the shotgun.

"They argued some. Shouted so loud a couple times that I could hear some of their noise. Couldn't make out what they were saying, of course, but I could hear the noise of it.

"Then Barrington, he draped the mail pouch over his shoulder and acted like he was gonna keep it.

"That's when the man with the shotgun pulled the trigger on him. Shot him in the belly and doubled him over.

"Barrington went down on his knees, holding himself the way a gutshot man will. He was looking at the man with the shotgun. The robber stepped over to him and took the mail pouch from him, then shoved the shotgun into his face and let off that other barrel.

"Cold son of a bitch, let me tell you." The Sharpshooter cackled. "We coulda used a man like that in the old days. Knock 'em dead. If he could use a rifle, that is. Killing a man close up with a scattergun, that don't mean shit. Killing from a quarter mile off, now that's something a man can be proud of."

If you say so, Longarm thought. But he didn't say it aloud. This poor miserable bastard had enough ghosts flittering through his brain. He didn't need any of Longarm's sass now too.

"Marshal," the Sharpshooter said.

"Yes?"

"I've been thinking it over, an' I've decided."

"What's that?"

"I don't expect I'd like spending time in a jail cell, all cooped up and strangers around me. I expect I'd rather go down like a man than let you do that to me."

With that the fellow whirled and leaped for his old Sharps sniper's rifle near the mouth of the cave.

Chapter 25

"Shit!" Longarm bawled.

He jumped too. The Sharpshooter jumped for his rifle and Longarm jumped for the Sharpshooter.

Damn the man anyway.

The Sharpshooter was by far the closer, but Longarm was the younger and the quicker.

The Sharpshooter reached the rifle first and grabbed it up, but Longarm was only half a step behind him and didn't even think about slowing his charge. He dipped his shoulder and came in low, beneath the swinging barrel of that long old Sharps, and threw himself full tilt into the Sharpshooter's midsection.

Both men went down. Hard. Longarm was on top, and heard a hoarse *whoosh* as the breath was driven out of the Sharpshooter's lungs.

The rifle went flying, clattering onto the rock floor of the cave and skittering away.

Longarm still had his Colt in hand. It hadn't occurred to him to shoot the Sharpshooter with it, never mind that that would have been the logical and sensible thing to do. Longarm hadn't consciously thought it out, but the simple fact was that this hermit who'd withdrawn himself from society was neither a threat nor a criminal, and Longarm did not want to bring him to harm.

On the other hand, Longarm's forbearance was not so great that he would volunteer to take a bullet just so he could preserve the Sharpshooter's hide.

Still, the man had had his chance to kill Longarm if he'd wanted. And he'd passed the opportunity by. It seemed only fair to return that favor now.

Not that the Sharpshooter probably thought of himself as being in receipt of any favors.

Having knocked the wind from him, Longarm followed that "favor" by clubbing him on the temple with the butt of the big Colt.

The Sharpshooter's eyes rolled back in his head and he ceased struggling. To the point that for several seconds there Longarm thought he'd gone and killed the fellow by accident.

He hadn't. Quite. The man was still breathing, even though it took Longarm a little while to be sure of that. Once he was, he returned the revolver to his holster and fetched out some handcuffs instead.

"You had the chance. You should've killed me."

"Didn't want to," Longarm told him. "Now shut up for a minute lest I burn these steaks. What is this anyway? It's too light a color to be deer meat, and it doesn't look like elk neither."

"Bear," the Sharpshooter told him. "It's good. Not as tasty as mountain lion, but I like it. And there's plenty of them up here to choose from. Goat's good too, but those sons of bitches are terrible hard to skin."

Longarm grunted and added some lard—bear grease it probably was—to the skillet before he poked a long-handled fork into the slabs of meat and turned them over to sear the other side. "Mind if I ask you a personal question?"

The Sharpshooter pondered that for a moment, then shrugged. "Go ahead."

"What's your name?"

"John."

"Last name?"

"Smith."

"All right, that will do."

"You gonna take these manacles off me now?"

"Nope."

"I can't eat with them on."

"Comes the time, I'll put irons on your ankles and chain one o' your hands to—I dunno—the handle of that trunk over there. Which hand d'you want free to eat with, John Smith?"

"This one." Smith splayed the fingers of his right hand.

"Fine. But I expect you can make do with the other hand instead." Longarm grinned at him. "Just to make things a little more awkward in case you get to feeling feisty again."

"You're a right bastard, you know that?"

"So I've been told." The grin returned. "More'n once maybe." He set the skillet off the coals and tried to drag the trunk over to where he had John Smith propped against the cave wall. The trunk was so heavy he couldn't budge it. Not even after he became aware that it was damn-all heavy and gave it all his strength. "How the hell did you get this thing up here?"

"Wasn't so heavy when I carried it up."

"Well, it's a bitch now. Store your bullet lead in it, do you?"

"I already told you what's in there."

"Sure. Gold. Now tell me what it really is," Longarm said.

Smith snorted. "Open it up and look. It isn't locked."

Longarm looked from the trunk to Smith and back again. He leaned down and unfastened the hasp that held the lid shut.

The trunk was a standard, flat-topped, military-style locker, smaller than a steamer trunk but not by a hell of a lot.

109

It was filled almost to the top with chunks of unprocessed but rich—even to Longarm's untrained eye—gold. Longarm had no idea what that much gold would be worth. Tens of thousands of dollars probably.

"Jesus!" he blurted out.

"I wasn't lying," Smith said proudly.

"No, I guess you weren't. Damn." Longarm dropped the lid shut, brought out a second pair of cuffs that he clipped around Smith's ankles, and then dragged the man over and set him on top of his trunk full of gold. "Don't get any ideas now," Longarm warned as he unlocked the manacle from Smith's left hand and refastened it inside the steel loop of the trunk hasp, leaving that hand free while the right was tethered now to more gold than two men and a boy would be able to carry.

"You aren't going to take my gold?"

"Nope."

"Why?"

"That's a stupid question. It isn't mine."

"It's mine, though."

"Yep."

"You aren't gonna ask me where I got it?"

"Nope."

"You don't think I stole it, do you?"

"No. It'd've been processed through a stamp mill if it belonged to some regular outfit. This is all raw ore. Rich, though. Damn near pure, most of it."

"I found a vug." Smith cackled. "Cleaned that son of a bitch out. Now I'm looking for another one."

"A man could live a lifetime and not spend all the gold you got in that trunk, Mr. Smith."

Smith didn't respond to that. It occurred to Longarm that Smith's reason for being up here was not gold. Gold was merely his excuse. The truth was that he had withdrawn from society. Probably because of all the killing he'd been asked to do on behalf of his country.

And at that it must have been harder on Smith and his fellow Sharpshooters—Longarm had heard of the outfit but never before met anyone who'd been a member of it—than on the run-of-the-mill soldier. The normal boy in blue, or in gray for that matter, spent most of his time waiting and bellyaching about having to wait. When he did fight, it was in long, scared rows of soldiers who ran and yelled and shot, but the enemy was generally just a line of anonymous figures dimly seen through a screen of powder smoke.

Smith and his companions went about their war like hunters in a thickly populated patch of squirrel woods, picking out one target at a time and deliberately extinguishing one human life after another.

That must have created a rather special sort of hell for those men, Longarm thought now.

No, it wasn't gold Smith was here to find. Which would certainly explain why he'd been so quick to offer it up when he thought Longarm was a robber come to call.

What the man really wanted was peace for his soul. Or forgiveness, which Longarm supposed was just another way of saying the same thing. Somehow he doubted the man would find that here.

Longarm found tin plates where Smith told him he would, then cut up the man's meat for him rather than allow the Sharpshooter a knife to cut his own. They ate in silence.

Just what, Longarm kept asking himself, was he supposed to do with this man now that he had the poor, sad son of a bitch?

Chapter 26

"You prob'ly haven't kept up with the news, being as you're away off to yourself up here."

"I go down to Leadville now an' then," Smith retorted.

"Slip in and buy a few things, then get back out in a hurry?"

"As a matter of fact that is the way I like it. Anything wrong with that?"

"No, Mr. Smith, there's not a thing wrong with that. I was just thinking you probably don't read the newspapers much."

"Don't read anything, not the papers nor books nor none of that. Never learned how."

Longarm could scarcely imagine not being able to read. He didn't say anything about that now, though. Especially since in Smith's case it was a lack that could be considered handy.

"Been some changes in the law since the war," Longarm told Smith as he was finishing washing their plates. "Lots of crime out this way and not much in the way of tax money to build prisons and like that."

"Why should I care about such as that, Marshal?" Smith asked.

"Because as a United States deputy marshal, Mr. Smith,

it is within my power to administer summary justice and make, um, arrangements for these sentences to be carried out in such a way as to benefit the taxpayers an' citizens of this here state."

"I got no idea what you just said," Smith admitted. That was all right. Longarm himself didn't have but a vague sort of idea about where this was heading.

"Yeah, well, I've decided not to charge you with assault on a peace officer. Which I could certainly do. Nor attempted murder. Which is lucky for you because that would be harder to prove and would have to go before a regular judge and jury.

"No, sir, Mr. Smith, I think I'll charge you with willful destruction of private property."

"That sounds bad, Marshal."

"It is bad, Mr. Smith. Willful destruction is a serious offense."

"How much time am I likely t' get for it?"

"Two years," Longarm said firmly. "That's the law."

Smith looked ready to cry. "I don't think I can do two years locked up with strangers, Marshal. You wouldn't kill me a while ago, but at least let me kill myself. I'm begging you. Just let me have my old rifle. Or my skinning knife if you don't trust me with the rifle. Not that I'd shoot you. I swear to God I wouldn't."

"I can't let you kill yourself, Smith. It'd look bad on my record if I was to allow a prisoner to escape from his just obligations to society like that."

"But . . ."

"No buts, Mr. Smith. I won't let you kill yourself an' that's that. Reckon what I will do is try you myself. I can do that right here under these summary-justice laws I was telling you about."

"But what about—?"

"Will you shut up an' listen to me for a minute, Mr. Smith? I'm gonna try you on a charge of"—he had to think fast in order to remember what foolishness he'd told Smith a minute ago—"willful destruction of another's pri-

114

vate property. To wit, a horse belonging to Mr. Alexander Dumont of Fairplay, Colorado."

Longarm cocked his head and aimed a finger at Smith. "I will be honest with you, Mr. Smith. I'm not only gonna try you, I'm gonna find your ass guilty, sir. Guilty as charged."

Smith swallowed. Hard.

"And once I've found you officially guilty, I am gonna impose sentence on you."

"Two years, you said?"

"Two years," Longarm agreed.

"I done told you, I couldn't stand to spend two years in prison."

"Remember I said this state is short on prison space, Smith. D'you remember me telling you that?"

"Yes, sir, I expect that I do."

"Good. Because I'm gonna sentence you to two years of non-penal public service."

"Non-what?"

"It means you won't be going to prison. You'll serve your two years right here, Mr. Smith."

Smith looked at the wrist that was handcuffed to the trunk full of gold, then looked up at Longarm. He looked confused. That was all right. Longarm was still working out the details of this deal himself.

"Your sentence, Mr. Smith, will be to watch over the goods and the persons moving over the Mosquito Pass road." Longarm aimed the finger again and in a stern voice solemnly said, "In particular, sir, you will be held responsible for the safety of the United States mails and all personnel affiliated with or pertaining to the United States Post Office. Am I making myself clear, sir?"

"Y-yes, sir. I expect you are."

"For two years, Mr. Smith. To the day. Oh, and you will be assessed restitution for the horse you killed."

"How much will that be?"

Longarm had less than no idea what a horse like that one would be worth. Still, better to make the amount large. Smith could afford it, what with his honking big trunk full of raw gold. And the more it cost, the better Smith would feel about having to pay it. In a left-handed sort of way, that is. Longarm figured he needed to put at least a little bitterness in the medicine, or the patient wouldn't think there was any benefit to taking it.

"Five hundred dollars," Longarm said in a crisp and he hoped official-sounding voice.

"Yes, sir, Marshal." Smith looked and sounded chastened. Good.

"Now lie down where you are there and get some sleep. We'll hold your trial in the morning."

"But . . ."

"This won't be official until we have the trial, Smith. And you won't be eligible for release into public service until you've been adjudicated guilty and formal sentence imposed."

"Yeah, I can understand that."

"Here. You can have the blanket and pillow off your bunk. But you got to stay chained to that trunk tonight."

"Yes, sir." The Sharpshooter looked genuinely contrite.

Now, Longarm thought, all he had to do was come up with some kind of ceremonial mumbo jumbo for the trial come daybreak.

Then he could get back to the serious business of finding a killer. Which once again was looking like Charlie Ellis. Or Campbell, as he seemed to be calling himself now.

Sure was a shame, though. He'd certainly thought the chase was over once he found John Smith's lair.

He sighed and went to tidying up so he too could stretch out and get some sleep.

After all, he had a trial to conduct in the morning and a felon to sentence.

He chuckled to himself just a little as he prepared to turn in.

Chapter 27

He was cutting things pretty close, really. Chasing a ghost from the recent war had eaten up his time so that he would have to hustle in order to intercept Ed Macklin for his first-of-the-month carry from Alma to Leadville.

This was the day Macklin should be making the leg of the journey that took him from the Widow Shreave's over the pass and down again to Barton's on the Leadville side.

Last week back at Shreave's Inn Longarm had assured Macklin that even if he hadn't yet found the killer's hide-out, he would be able to position himself between there and the pass and that the killer couldn't possibly reach Ed Macklin without going through Custis Long beforehand.

At the time it'd seemed a sensible enough plan. Longarm had fully expected to have Barrington's killer in hand once he ran the rifleman to earth. And a fine plan it had been too. Except, that is, for the fact that it started off with a false premise when he assumed that John Smith was the robber and the killer. That poor, gullible son of a bitch wasn't either of those things.

Now Smith was back in his cave preparing to serve out his public-service "sentence" after Longarm had tried and convicted him early in the morning. That was all to the good so far as it went. Unfortunately it didn't do anything

117

toward putting a noose around the actual killer's neck.

Longarm had hurried through the mock trial, bummed a slab of bear meat from Smith—the man had insisted that his name really was John Smith—and begun hauling ass out to the Mosquito Pass road as quick as he could manage.

He got there late in the forenoon, and decided rather than waiting in Smith's very useful hiding place, it would be better to slip back down on the Alma side so as to intercept Macklin on the letter carrier's way up.

Longarm figured Macklin to reach the summit of the pass about noon, and it would have been easiest for Longarm simply to wait there and meet him. The problem with that was that Longarm didn't know where the robber would choose to strike on this trip. It could be in or beyond the pass. But it could as easily be somewhere between Shreave's and the summit. Longarm didn't figure he could afford to make any more wrong assumptions here and so he should get himself into position to help Macklin as early as possible.

Late as Longarm was in reaching the road, the robber might very well already be in position to strike. He could be lurking behind any rock or in any aspen copse or tangle of scrub oak.

Longarm was tempted to try to keep out of sight while slipping along parallel to the road. Then it occurred to him that the robber would be waiting for, and would recognize, Ed Macklin. But a total stranger coming from the opposite direction would arouse no interest whatsoever.

It would be quicker and more sensible for Longarm to simply hike along the middle of the road in plain sight until he met up with Macklin. Then he could turn sneaky.

So once he scrambled down the hillside to the road, he laid his Winchester over his right shoulder and began striding downhill with a vacant expression and whistling a gay tune. No, sir, he was just as innocent a traveler as anybody could ever hope to be. You bet.

Chapter 28

Longarm walked. And kept on walking. Through the noon, through the afternoon, and through more swarms of mosquitoes than he could count. Hell, it was the swarms that he lost track of. He couldn't even imagine the number of individual bloodsucking little sons of bitches that feasted on his blood.

And none of that bloodletting accomplished a damn thing.

Not only did he fail to see the Mosquito Range killer, he failed to find Ed Macklin too.

In the late afternoon Longarm rounded another of the innumerable kinks in the road to see below him a quarter mile or so the unmistakable stone wall and smoking chimneys that marked Agnes Shreave's inn.

And still no Macklin.

He could, he supposed, have miscalculated the days. Off in the mountains seeking out John Smith and his cave ... sure, that was probably it. He'd simply lost track of the calendar, a concept that was meaningless in mountains like that, so more than likely Macklin wasn't due until tomorrow.

That should present no problem. He'd just get a good rest tonight—he could use one after all this hiking—and tomorrow get on with the business of finding Fitz Barrington's murderer.

Having decided that, he quickened his steps and hurried the rest of the way down to the ramshackle inn.

"What the hell d'you mean he was here already?" Longarm was feeling decidedly testy at the news, and his pique put a harsh edge on his normal, easygoing tone of voice.

"Just what I said, of course," the Widow Shreave snapped right back at him. "Ed got here yesterday right on schedule. In a real good humor too, everything considered. I mean, you know, what with him expecting to be robbed this trip. He acted nervous but not too scared. Got up extra early this morning and took off out of here . . . it must've been three o'clock when he left out of here. Didn't even wait for us to cook anything for him.

"I heard him moving around and came out to see what was up . . . a lady can't be too careful, you know, what with strangers staying in the place and everything, so I sleep light. Offered to cook something for him, but he said he wanted to get away. I gave him some leftover biscuits and a chunk of cold meat to take with him, and he went on.

"By now he'll be over at Barton's, I'm sure. I'm surprised you didn't see him on your way down here."

"So am I," Longarm admitted glumly.

Dammit. He'd wasted time with that playacting trial for John Smith. Maybe if he'd gotten up and gone over to the pass first thing in the morning . . .

Fuck it! "Maybe" was one useless sonuvabitch of a word. "Maybe" wouldn't feed the dog. And "maybe" damn sure wouldn't catch the killer. A man who fretted about "maybe" this or "maybe" that was just "maybe-ing" away his opportunities to accomplish something. That was a game Longarm did not want to start playing. What he had to do now was get on with correcting the problem rather than sitting around worrying about how it'd happened.

"You'll be wanting your same room tonight, Marshal?" Mrs. Shreave asked him.

"Yes, ma'am, I expect that I will."

She gave him a smile. "I'll have the girls make sure it's ready for you then."

He thanked her and, his feet sore and his neck and hands a mass of itching welts from all the mosquito bites, turned to go find himself a drink and some supper.

Tomorrow, thank goodness, would be another day.

Chapter 29

"Oh, my," Horace Barton said when Longarm introduced himself. "Your name is Long, you say?"

"Uh-huh."

"Deputy marshal, are you?"

"Uh-huh."

"Oh, my," the Leadville-side innkeeper said with a cluck of the tongue and a shake of his graying head. "Oh, my."

"Something wrong?" Longarm asked.

"Not with me, no, sir. Not anything wrong here at all. But I got to tell you, mister, Ed Macklin is mighty pissed off at you right now. Oh, my." He shook his head again.

"What happened?" Longarm asked. Not that he had to ask, really. He knew what it pretty much had to be if Macklin was upset.

"Got robbed again, of course. Oh, my. And he was counting on you to be there and protect him, oh, yes." Horace Barton sighed. And shook his head. The man needed a haircut, Longarm decided. All that hair swayed and bobbed when he shook his head like that. Longarm did wish Barton would quit shaking his damn head.

Horace Barton looked at Longarm again and wordlessly shook his head. Longarm felt like punching him.

"D'you want to tell me about it?" Longarm asked.

"Better you should wait and talk to Ed, don't you think? He'll be back up here tomorrow night."

"I don't mean the details," Longarm said. "Just . . ."

Barton shook his head. And sighed. That was becoming a mite tiresome too. "All I know for sure, mister, is that Ed got robbed again. And he's awful pissed off about you not being there when he was."

"Same robber, was it?"

"I don't think Ed asked to see the gent's credentials—" Longarm was beginning to believe that Horace Barton was something of a smart-ass—"but it appeared to've been the same fellow who pulled all those other robberies. Or so I'm led to believe."

Longarm shook his head—damned if it wasn't catching—and grunted.

"You want a room for tonight, mister?"

"Yes, I expect I do, thank you."

"Two dollars for yourself and your horse."

"No horse," Longarm corrected him.

Barton gave him an odd look. But didn't comment. And didn't shake his head this time. Longarm deeply appreciated that. "One dollar that would be then," Barton amended. "Meals are extra."

"All right, thanks."

"If you're horny, I got a fat little Ute squaw that'll do for you. She isn't much to look at, but she's a warm place to put it and better than some. Only a dollar extra. If you want her, though, let me know now so's you can get early in line. There's three fellows in front of you now. And to show you my heart's in the right place, mister, I can put the charge for her on the government voucher for payment. Won't have to come outa your pocket that way."

Longarm was horny. Neither of the Shreave girls had visited his room last night. But he damn sure wasn't *that* horny. "I appreciate the offer, Mr. Barton, but I reckon I'll pass on it. I'm pretty tired after all the walking. Y'know?"

"Whatever you like."

"Say, while I think about it, have you seen this man?" Longarm pulled out his little folio of photographs and offered them to Barton for inspection. "His name is Ellis," Longarm said, "but he may be calling himself Campbell now."

Barton looked at the pictures one by one, then reversed the order and went through them a second time. After a bit he shook his head. "I don't have much of a memory for faces, and that's the natural truth. Seems to me this fella looks just the least bit familiar to me, but I can't say for certain sure. He might've come through here. Might've not. I'm just not for sure."

"All right. Thanks." Longarm tucked the pictures away again. "You said something about meals?" He hadn't had anything to eat since breakfast back at Shreave's Inn and his belly was growling. The hunger was almost annoying enough to make him forget about the itching of his mosquito bites. And that fact made skipping supper almost a temptation. Almost, that is.

"In there," Barton said, pointing. "Twenty-five cents for potluck—which, I can tell you, is stew made from whatever's left over lately—or forty cents if you want a proper meal. That would be elk roast, gravy, and rice."

"I'll take the roast. You can put it on the voucher if you please."

"Whatever suits you, mister. Whatever suits you."

Longarm thanked the man and went to turn away. "Oh, my," he heard Barton mutter. Longarm didn't have to look around to see what the man was doing when he said that. He already knew. Barton would be shaking his damned head again.

Chapter 30

Come the morning, Longarm was feeling decidedly out of sorts. He'd slept poorly on a mattress that was hard and lumpy and filled with small crawling things, and to top that off, his breakfast—for which Barton was charging the United States taxpayers a whole quarter—consisted of a choice between a bowl of hot cornmeal mush with molasses poured over it, or a plate full of fried cornmeal mush . . . with molasses poured over it. It wasn't that Longarm had anything against mush. Hell, he liked it most of the time. But for twenty-five cents a man ought to be fed better than that.

Not that his opinion was asked.

He finished his mush and an extra cup of coffee and pondered the next step.

He could sit right there and wait a few hours and Ed Macklin would come to him. Or he could hike on down toward Leadville and meet Macklin partway down the mountain.

Longarm decided to move on down the trail. Quite aside from the fact that a little privacy might be in order when Macklin cussed him out for having let the robber strike again unopposed, Longarm simply didn't much care for the idea of sitting idly on his ass when there were things to be done.

He gathered up his gear, bought a fat panatela to supplement his dwindling supply of cheroots, and started down toward the Arkansas River valley far below.

"Damn you," Macklin grumbled when he and Longarm met near the bottom of the Mosquito Pass road.

"I'm sorry," Longarm told him. "I thought I had our man. Turned out I was wrong." He motioned Macklin off the trail and gave the man a smoke by way of a peace offering. The depth of his apology was displayed in the fact that he gave Macklin one of his own fine cheroots, and not Horace Barton's urine-soaked hunk of old rope that the man passed off as a panatela.

Longarm briefly explained about John Smith. "He was watching that day Barrington was killed, even described it all for me. But I'm convinced he wasn't the man that did it, if only because it was a shotgun that was used. I wouldn't say that Smith is actually proud of having been a Sharpshooter. If anything, he's disgusted with himself over it. But if he was going to kill someone, it would've been with that rifle, not a scattergun."

"Oh, I can believe he isn't your man. After all, while you were up there visiting with him, the robber was down on the road scaring the crap out of me," Macklin said.

"I'd appreciate it if you'd tell me what happened."

Macklin puffed on his cheroot for a moment, presumably gathering his thoughts and perhaps quelling some of his anger with Longarm at the same time, then said, "I left extra early that morning. Since I hadn't seen you at the inn, I assumed you were along the road watching out for me, and I guess I was more than a little anxious to get this over and done with."

"That's understandable," Longarm said.

"Anyway, I took off from the inn real early. Mrs. Shreave was awake. She was in the kitchen doing whatever it is women do in the middle of the night to get

128

breakfast started. Making biscuits or something, I'd guess. Anyway, she came out and spoke to me. Made me up a packet of leftovers from the night before, and saw me out so's she could bar the door again once I was on my way."

Macklin made a low, growling sound deep in his throat. "Marshal, I hadn't gone half a mile—hell, less than that— before the robber stepped out of the brush square in front of me.

"Scared me half to death, I don't mind telling you. I mean, here it was still black as a lawyer's soul, the air cold and crisp and everything quiet. Then I heard this crackling in the bushes on the side of the road. Well, I thought it was an elk or big mule deer. Noisy, you know? Couldn't have been a bear or a painter cat. It was too noisy for either of them.

"So I stopped and . . . like . . . waited for whatever it was to cross the road. Like I said, I figured it was an elk and I didn't want to get stompled or something. Bunch of damn elk get spooky, they can trample a man to death by pure accident. You know?"

Longarm nodded.

"So I stopped and waited, but what climbed up onto the damn road was my robber. Son of a bitch was panting and wheezing . . . and pointing that shotgun at my belly.

"I guess I damn near got lucky when I left the inn so early. He must've been hiding someplace near but wasn't yet ready for me. Had to hurry and catch up when I walked past him never knowing he was there. My tough luck that he spotted me and was able to climb straight up between the switchbacks to get in front of me like he did. But he did it, all right, and before I knew what was what, he was standing there with that same damn shotgun.

"Let me tell you, though, I didn't want to end up like Barrington did, so when he waved the muzzles toward the mule, I didn't hesitate. I dumped my pouch just as quick as I could get the thing loose. Dropped it right there in the road like I done before more than once and stepped back away from it." Macklin puffed on his smoke and said, "You'd think a body would get used to this sort of thing, but I haven't. Don't want to neither."

"You were saying?" Longarm prompted.

"Yeah, well, after I dropped my mail pouch, the ol' robber, he nodded and motioned with the gun again to tell me to get on out of there. And believe me, I did that. Took up the lead rope of my mule and moved along quick as the two of us could go.

"I kept looking around for you, Marshal. Kept hoping you'd step out too, or anyway, that I'd hear a gunshot behind me there to tell me you'd been watching over me like I expected you to do. I knew you hadn't been there when I got down on this side of the summit. Looked back toward the pass and seen you coming down the mountainside from somewhere up high there. That's when I knew you hadn't been in position down toward Shreave's where the robber found me this time.

"I was pretty mad at you, Marshal. I'm telling you that right out. But . . . I've had a couple days to think it over. I know you've done your best. And you can't be everywhere."

For a brief instant it crossed Longarm's mind that Ed Macklin could be the robber himself and was making all this up.

Then, just as quickly, he remembered that there was a witness. John Smith. And Macklin hadn't known anything about him. Smith not only corroborated Macklin's story, he added details to it that Macklin couldn't have known about.

So much for that stillborn idea.

"I think," Longarm said slowly, forming the idea even as the words came out of his mouth, "I think we need to fix it so your robber will strike again before next month's first carry."

"Marshal, are you outa your damn mind?" Macklin yelped. "I don't want to bait that bastard into more robbing. I want to stop him."

"And that's exactly what I have in mind, Ed. Trust me."

130

"Like I did this trip?"

"That's right. Exactly like that." Longarm gave the man a long, level look.

Ed Macklin grumbled and groused for a minute or two. Then, reluctantly, he nodded. "Tell me what you want me to do. I want shut of this problem so bad I expect I'll do it if I can."

"Thank you, Ed. And what I'm wanting won't be hard." He smiled. "Not the first part of it anyhow. After that, well, we'll just have to see does it work."

Chapter 31

What with one distraction after another, darkness caught him still on the road. Longarm bedded down that night beside the narrow, racing upper reaches of the Arkansas, and slept with the sound of rushing water for music and a canopy of bright stars for a ceiling. He'd spent nights under worse conditions, and that was for damn sure.

Come morning, he hiked the rest of the way up the valley to Leadville. He could hear the town and smell it long before he could see it. The upper valley was filled with the thud of stamp mills operating and the acid stink of chemicals as the silver ores were reduced from rock to metal.

It was a funny thing, but Leadville had almost died a premature death when the gold veins of the original discovery played out. Not only did the gold yield diminish, but the mines had to contend with the nuisance of some blue-colored crap that kept clogging the mills.

It wasn't until people had started drifting away from the town that someone discovered that all the annoying blue shit was exceptionally rich silver ore. And Leadville boomed for a second time.

The town was still going strong now, gold forgotten here and silver reigning as king.

To Longarm's mind, one of the better things about it, though, was that down here they were relatively free from the swarms of mosquitoes he'd passed through on his way down from the pass. Down here he could walk and breathe and even unbutton his coat, and not have to worry about being picked up and carried away on ten thousand tiny wings. Miserable little sons of bitches!

The first place he stopped once he hit the business district was a cafe, where he filled up on real food. Pork chops, fried potatoes, and a slab of pie made with canned cherries and swimming in cream so rich it was yellow with butter. He felt considerably better once he wrapped himself around that.

Next stop was the first barber he came across for a haircut and a bath.

Finally, presentable in public once again and with his belly full, he looked up the post office.

"I'm looking for Postmaster Herren," Longarm announced to the stocky, one-armed man behind the counter.

"That'd be me."

Longarm introduced himself, only to feel a definite chill in the air—one that had nothing to do with the temperature outside—when Herren realized that this was the deputy who'd let Macklin down.

Longarm offered no explanations. If the postmaster didn't like things, fuck him. Longarm didn't figure he owed the man anything. He did, however, mention to Herren that no serious harm was done when the Mosquito Range robber took Ed Macklin's pouch this latest time.

"The postmaster over to Alma knows what to expect, y'know," Longarm confided. "He figured that pouch would be lost, so all the really valuable mail was held back. It'll come over in next week's carry."

"Ed didn't mention anything about that," Herren said.

"He was prob'ly so pissed off at me for missing the robbery that he never thought to. He'll tell you about it next Wednesday, I'm sure. That's when you can expect the bulk of what should've been this week's carry."

"Yeah, well, sure." Herren did not sound appreciably friendlier.

A couple of patrons in the place gave Longarm a critical looking-over the same as their postmaster did. Fuck them too, Longarm figured.

"Is there something you want, Deputy?" Herren said.

"As a matter of fact, yes." Longarm pulled out Charlie Ellis's photos and laid them on the counter. "D'you know this man?" He and Macklin had a plan of sorts, but if he could find Ellis and wrap this up before Macklin started out on his next trip, well, so much the better.

Herren inspected the pictures, but shook his head when he was done with them. "Nope," he said. "I can't swear he's never posted anything here, but he certainly doesn't have a box in this post office, and I don't recall him ever coming in to pick up anything by general delivery."

"All right, thanks." Longarm turned to the other patrons and offered them the photos too. One of the men barely bothered to glance in the direction of the images, but two others were courteous enough to give them a careful going-over.

"No, sorry," the first said. "I don't recall seeing this fella before."

"Me neither."

"All right. Thanks."

From the post office Longarm ambled on, stopping at a mercantile, where he bought a handful of decent cheroots that were almost as good a quality as he could find back home in Denver. Then to a saloon, where he replenished his traveling supply of Maryland rye whiskey. To another store, where he bought some sulfur-tipped lucifers and a cunning little brass case to keep them in, the case being warranted waterproof by the manufacturer. To a saloon, where he enjoyed a drink and some conversation with the men who were relaxing there. To the boarding-house where Ed Macklin always stayed, so Longarm could arrange for a room too.

In each of these places he showed Charlie Ellis's pictures and chatted with anyone who would give him the courtesy of listening.

Finally he looked up a livery stable where he could hire a saddle horse. Which wasn't all that easy in Leadville. Miners had notoriously little use for saddle stock, and the first two stables Longarm inquired at had only heavy draft horses, some buggies to rent, and—far and away their most common commodity—burros suitable for working in the underground drifts and adits where they normally pulled the ore carts that ran on track laid deep inside the mines.

"I'll be using your animal for a couple days," Longarm told the hostler, "then I'll send him back down to you."

"You aren't going prospecting way the hell and gone off the road, are you?" the liveryman demanded.

"No, sir. It's just that I've walked s' damn much lately I've got to get my boots resoled soon as I get home. I'm just plain tired of walking an' want to fork a decent horse again." Longarm rather balefully eyed the nag that was the best—and only—mount the stable had to offer, then amended that statement to: "Well, anyway, I want to be on a horse again. Forget I said anything about decent."

"You don't have to take him if'n you don't want," the hostler said.

"I want him," Longarm responded quickly lest the man take offense and withdraw the rental.

"All right then."

"I'll pick him up first thing tomorrow."

"He'll be saddled and ready for you by break of day, mister."

Longarm handed over a government voucher for the man to submit and for Henry eventually to pay, then headed back to the boardinghouse, where it would soon be time for supper.

When he thought of Henry and the office, it occurred to him that there was a telegraph line through to Leadville. There was still time enough this afternoon that he could

136

find it and get a wire off to Billy Vail, bringing the boss up to date.

But then, hell, there wasn't much progress to report. Yet. And besides, it wouldn't do to get Billy spoiled to the idea that he should expect reports while Longarm was operating in the field.

Better to let things lie and not stir up any snakes' nests.

Besides, it'd been a spell now since that late breakfast, and he was more than ready to eat again. He lengthened his stride and hurried on to the boardinghouse.

Chapter 32

After supper—filling, but cheap and starchy, as a body might expect at a boardinghouse with a transient clientele—Longarm sat for a few minutes on the front porch enjoying a cheroot while his meal settled, then excused himself from the dullards who'd shared the dining room table and walked back downtown with his packet of photographs to show around.

It was work, wasn't it? And that certainly qualified the evening as a legitimate expense. On the way to the nearest saloon, he reminded himself that this time he really must remember to ask for receipts for his purchases. Sure he would!

The first place he came to was the Wee Gordy. Next to it was the Black Swan. Beyond that one the Bell and Whistle. He was beginning to get the idea that Leadville was the sort of town a drinking man could learn to love.

If he could stand the cold, that is. Here it was the middle of summer and once the sun went down, the air became purely frigid. Longarm turned his coat collar up and stuffed his hands into his pockets until he gained the yeasty warmth of the Wee Gordy.

• • •

"No, sir. Sorry."

"Nope."

"Not me."

"Go fuck yourself, lawdog; I don't have t' put up with any o' your shit." That one, Longarm guessed, had done some time behind bars. And probably at the penitentiary level and not just some small-town local jail.

"Sorry, Marshal, no, I haven't seen him either."

Saloon after saloon brought the same set of disappointing—but not entirely unexpected—results.

Until he reached a place called the Monkey Nuts—the sign outside just said Monkey, but another indoors, where only men would read it, added the rest of the name, along with a wall painting with a wildly exaggerated depiction of a monkey's cods—where the customers seemed slightly different.

It took Longarm a few minutes to make out what the difference was here. Then it dawned on him. The Monkey Nuts crowd was silent.

Everywhere else he'd been this evening, the drinkers were there to have a good time.

In the Monkey Nuts the men seemed intent on the task of pouring whiskey down their gullets with swift and solemn determination. They acted more like the whiskey was medicine than pleasure. And come to think of it, nearly all the glasses in sight were whiskey glasses and not beer mugs.

These boys were plumb serious about their pursuit of stupor.

They also seemed a little better dressed, and certainly had more money in their pockets than the run-of-the-mine gents he'd been seeing in the other bars.

The name of the place finally tipped him. Monkeys. As in powder monkeys. These were boys who spent their working hours tempting the vagaries of fate and giant powder. A moment's carelessness, a tiny scrape of steel against hard stone—these men never knew when they went underground in the morning if they would be alive to walk out again come the end of their shift.

The one thing they knew for certain sure was that if they ever did fuck up, there wouldn't be a burial. Or if there was, they could use a matchbox for the coffin. There wouldn't be anything more than that left over to scrape up and mumble over.

No wonder it was so quiet in here, Longarm thought.

He almost excused himself and backed out of the place. But by the time he realized what was up he'd already ordered a drink—a beer, which immediately called attention to him in here—and helped himself to a pickled egg off the free-lunch plate. He might as well stay long enough to have a sip of the beer and drag the photos out one last time.

This time, though, much to his surprise, he got a flicker of recognition when he showed his pictures of Charlie Ellis/Campbell.

"I think . . . I'm not for sure now, but I think I've seen this fella before. Give me a minute and I'll try and remember where that woulda been, mister."

Chapter 33

Fat Ass Stella. He could see why they called her that. The woman had an ass on her that a Percheron mare would envy. The funny thing was that the rest of her body was relatively normal in size and shape. Well, except for the fact that she had tits the size and shape of watermelons. But her torso and arms were pretty normal.

That ass, though. An ax handle wide and then some, he guessed. Without exaggeration. He would've enjoyed knowing the actual measurement just for purposes of amazement. He'd honest to Pete never in his life seen an ass like that on any human person. Until now.

"Leticia said you wanted to see me?" she growled by way of greeting.

"Yes, ma'am." Longarm held his Stetson meekly before him and tried to act properly respectful. Which wasn't necessarily easy when the other party was a whorehouse madam who didn't actually deserve any respect. Still, Longarm reminded himself, he was a public servant, and Fat Ass Stella was a member of that public.

"What for?" she demanded.

Longarm introduced himself and hauled out the pictures of Charlie Ellis. He'd had so much practice lately that he could get those photos out damn near as slick as he could palm his Colt. "I'm trying to locate this gentleman so he can help me clear up a case I'm working on, ma'am."

Fat Ass Stella took the pictures and sniffed a few times as she examined them, first one and then another and finally the third. She went through them a second time, holding them close to her nose and peering at them extra carefully. When she was done with all that, she handed them back to Longarm. "Don't know him," was all she said.

"Are you sure about that, ma'am? I'm told—that is, I am given to understand—that the gentleman is a customer of yours."

"Then somebody told you wrong. I don't know him." Her voice was cold and flat and brooked no argument.

"Yes, ma'am. Thank you." He returned the photos in their pasteboard folios to his coat pocket.

Longarm looked past the middle-aged madam to the parlor, where half a dozen young women in flimsy kimonos and plenty of face paint and cheap perfume were competing for the attention of the two customers in the place. "Are those real Cuban cigars the, um, ladies are offering, ma'am?"

"Same thing. I get 'em out of someplace down in the islands called Tampa. Smoke them myself. They're good."

"Sell them, do you?"

"Sell them, yes. Give them, no. You may be a copper, Marshal, but you're no Leadville copper and I don't owe you shit. If you want anything here you'll pay for it same as anybody else. Cigars, whiskey, pussy, whatever."

"That's fine, ma'am." He'd had enough whiskey for one evening, and the idea of sticking his dick into one of the pasty-faced, sick-looking whores in this house wouldn't have appealed to him on his worst day. But earlier in the evening he'd finished the last of his cheroots, and the thought of a decent smoke was almighty enticing.

"Ten cents," Fat Ass told him. "Don't try and wheedle

the price down. My girls don't give out charity unless I tell them."

"Yes, ma'am."

"And stop trying to butter me up with all that 'ma'am' bullshit. I know what everybody in town calls me. Just don't you nor any other son of a bitch call me that to my face. Do you hear me?"

"Yes, ma'am."

"Margie! Fetch this gentleman the cigar tray."

Longarm went into the parlor, where a very drunk man wearing a coat and tie was trying to decide between a redhead and a blonde—the fellow eventually realized he couldn't choose one over the other and so took both of them upstairs—while the other potential customer was trying to get a girl with big tits but no other apparent qualifications to give him a free feel.

A scrawny young woman with young skin but aged and lifeless eyes brought the cigar tray to him. Fat Ass might be a lot of things, Longarm thought, but she knew how to stock cigars. This was as fine a selection as he could have found in Denver . . . and not so very many places there would be able to match it.

"I think . . . a few of these," Longarm said, scooping a handful of pale, perfect cigars from a wooden box with the words Garcia y Garcia burnt into the lid.

"That'll be a dollar, mister."

Margie obviously wanted to extract a little something for herself out of this deal, he thought; he'd only taken eight cigars out of the box. Rather than start a fuss over nothing, he handed the bawd a dollar.

"You want the cutter, mister?"

"Yes, and a candle to warm and light it too."

She took the tray away, and returned a moment later with another, smaller silver tray that had several implements to choose from, including a cigar warmer with the candle already lighted. Longarm carefully nipped the tight, dry twist at the end of his smoke, and began passing it slowly back and forth above the candle flame.

His concentration was interrupted by a loud crash from the entrance hall and an excited yelp in a woman's voice.

Longarm looked up but did not rise. Whorehouse brawls were best left to whorehouse bouncers, he'd always figured.

There was more shouting, a little loud cussing—this in a man's voice—and some more thumping and banging. It sounded like someone was falling down the steps.

"Oh, Jesus!" Margie shrieked, drawing Longarm's attention to her. She was staring toward the doorway from the parlor to the hall.

He looked too, naturally enough. And very nearly blurted out a comment similar to Margie's.

A whore he hadn't seen before was standing in the doorway there. She was bare-ass naked. Except for a thick and ever-growing stain of blood that started at her throat and spread down over her pale body.

He could see plain as plain could be the raw, gaping hole where somebody'd slit the girl's throat. She staggered, bumped into the side of the doorframe, and collapsed there.

The other girls in the room moved quickly toward her, but Longarm was quicker, striding past the blood-smeared girl—the other whores could tend to her, and likely do it better than Longarm would've been able to anyway—and on into the hall, where he could now see Fat Ass Stella shrinking back away from a man at the foot of the stairs.

The man, a well-groomed gent with gray hair and a handsomely trimmed beard, had a hawk-bill knife in his hand. Apart from the knife, he too was naked as a peeled egg.

"Bitch!" he was snarling as he tried to disembowel Fat Ass with a sweep of the knife. "You cunt. You put her up to it, didn't you?"

He swung the knife again. Fat Ass Stella tried to back away from him. Her heel caught on the rug and she tumbled backward onto the cheeks of her own enormous ass.

The man with the knife sprang forward, obviously in-

146

tending to finish on Stella what he'd started on the girl.

Longarm reached him before he could reach Stella, however.

When the knife hand lashed out, Longarm's hand was there to block it. He grasped the man's wrist in a vice-like grip and twisted.

"Hey!"

Longarm squeezed.

"I . . . damn you, you're hurting me." The stupid son of a bitch sounded like he didn't consider that to be quite fair. And never mind what he himself had just been doing. "Let go."

"Drop the knife."

"I'll cut your fucking heart out."

"Right," Longarm said dryly. And squeezed harder, this time applying all the pressure he could manage. He heard a sharp, distinctive snap as bone gave way inside the man's wrist, and the fellow screamed. The knife fell clattering to the floor.

"Damn you, you . . ." He didn't have time to finish whatever it was he wanted to say. Longarm let go of the man's wrist and tried to bury his own right-hand elbow deep in the fellow's gut.

That doubled him over, and Longarm stepped half a pace back, took his time measuring the exact placement that he wanted . . . and kicked the piece of shit square on the point of his jaw.

Once more there was the dull crunch of breaking bone.

This time, though, the man didn't cry out. He was unconscious before he had time to scream again.

Longarm grunted with disgust, then helped a trembling and obviously terrified Fat Ass Stella to her feet.

Chapter 34

"Who is this piece of rancid shit?" Longarm asked as he finished putting iron on the naked man's wrists and ankles.

Stella shuddered. "His name is Jeremy Beitlinger. He's a town councilman. He . . . he's always been rough on the girls. Likes to beat them up. But . . . never anything like this before."

"I'd hope not."

"You might as well take those bracelets off him, Marshal. The law won't punish him."

Longarm grinned at her. "Want to make a bet on that?"

"Not here, it won't."

Longarm shrugged. "If not here, then in federal court down in Denver. And don't you worry about what charge he'd be tried on. I'm sure I can come up with something if I set my mind to it."

"Ma'am?" One of the girls was standing there tugging at Fat Ass Stella's sleeve.

"Yes, Wanda?"

"It's about Daisy, ma'am. He didn't cut the big vein in her neck, ma'am. It'll take her some time to heal up, but I think she'll be all right again. It looked an awful lot

149

worse than it is 'cause of all the blood. But she wasn't cut all that deep, thank goodness."

"Thank you, Wanda. Can you and Margie get her bandaged up and put to bed, please?"

"Yes, ma'am."

"And does Jezebel still have her street clothes on?"

"Yes'm, I think so."

"Good. Tell her she's to run fetch the chief of police."

"What if she's changed back into her kimono, ma'am?"

With exaggerated patience Stella instructed the girl, "Then please tell her to get dressed again. Then she's to bring Wally here. Can you remember all that, dear?"

"Yes, ma'am, I can, thank you." The girl hurried away, and Stella turned to Longarm and added, "Sometimes we're asked to make, um, house calls."

"I see."

"Gentlemen who don't want to be seen in a shitty place like this."

"Yes, of course," Longarm told her. He didn't know why she felt like she needed to make any explanations now. She'd been snotty enough before. Now she acted like Longarm was an old friend.

Well, maybe not an old friend. But a good one.

The Negro maid who'd let Longarm in earlier appeared now from the back of the house with a bucket and mop, and began cleaning up the mess left behind from all the bleeding. She pushed the mop around Councilman Beitlinger as if it wasn't a man lying there but a piece of furniture. And a piece of furniture that she didn't mind bumping and pummeling, at that.

"I'm thirsty, Marshal," Stella said. "Can I offer you something?"

"No, I'm fine, thanks."

"Well, I want something. Join me in my office?" She paused and then emphasized, "Please?"

Longarm relented. "Sure." He smiled. "Wouldn't want t' be rude to a lady, ma'am."

Fat Ass Stella snorted and rolled her eyes. Then she

150

laughed. "You wouldn't be Irish, would you, Marshal?"

"Not that I know of."

"Then you best look closer. Anyone with that much blarney in him is surely Irish. Come along. Lady, the man says." She rolled her eyes heavenward.

Stella started toward the back of the house, then turned and said, "Leticia, when Chief Dorn gets here, make sure he sees me and the marshal here before he does anything with Councilman Beitlinger."

"Yes, ma'am."

Just to make sure the good councilman stayed where he was, Longarm unfastened one of his ankle restraints and relocked it with the son of a bitch's legs tethered around the stairway banister. Beitlinger was beginning to regain consciousness. He started to groan and whine, so Longarm kicked him in the temple to put him under again. They didn't need his noise along with everything else.

"Are you coming, Marshal?"

"Yes, ma'am."

Fat Ass Stella's office was small and bare, entirely utilitarian, with a desk, three ladder-back chairs, and a cabinet. She motioned Longarm into one of the chairs, while she took another beside his rather than going behind the desk as he would have expected.

"I thought you wanted a drink," he said once it became obvious that that was not her intention.

"I wanted the girls to hear me invite you for a drink. God knows what-all they blabber to their johns." She shook her head. "Whores are stupid, Marshal. Don't ever think otherwise. If they think a client likes them for anything other than their twats, they lose all sense and can't be trusted. And if there is anything I don't need, mister, it's a rumor that a man's secrets aren't safe in Fat Ass Stella's joint." She grinned and added, "I told you I know what they call me. That's all right. I don't mind. Not considering the size of the bank balance I keep down in Denver. The thing is, I want that account to keep on growing. You know?"

151

"I'm beginning to," he said.

"I pay my debts, Marshal, and the one thing I can give you that I think you'll appreciate is a straight answer about the man in those photographs you showed me."

It was his turn to grin. "What? Surely you don't mean you lied to me a while ago."

"Hell, no, I didn't lie. But I've had a miraculous recovery of memory in the past few minutes."

"That works for me, Stella. And don't worry. No one has to know you've told me anything."

"The fella's name is Charlie Ellis. Calls himself Charlie Campbell nowadays, but the name was Ellis when he served time in Leavenworth. I take it you know about that?"

Longarm nodded. "I do."

"I don't know what you want Charlie for this time, Marshal, but I'm telling you straight out that whatever it is, he didn't do it. He's a good man. Comes in here twice a month, just as regular as my spinster sister's vapors—which she has every afternoon at four o'clock and can't manage without she has a few sips of Professor Dahl's Bitter Tonic—and never causes no trouble. The girls all love the man. He's clean and polite—unlike some, as you have cause to know already—and only asks for a girl to treat him decent. They all do. Wouldn't a one of them do any dirt to our Charlie, or the other girls would pull her hair out one at a time. And when her head was bald, they'd start on the pussy hair next. No, sir, we like Charlie here, and I'm telling you there isn't an indecent bone in that man's body."

"I'm not saying he's the man I'm after, Stella, but I need to talk to him. It's important."

She nodded. "I already made up my mind to tell you, Marshal. It just grieves me, that's all. You'll treat Charlie decent, will you?"

"I've never yet killed a man without cause. I guess I won't start with your friend. If he doesn't give me trouble, Stella, I'll treat him as decent as I know how."

"I accept your word for that."

They were interrupted by Leticia's tapping on the door. "Chief Dorn is here, ma'am."

Longarm stood and went out to find a very pissed-off chief of police. Pissed off because his old-fashioned manacle key wouldn't fit Longarm's tempered-steel handcuff locks. Otherwise Longarm's prisoner likely would have disappeared into the night.

It took Longarm a little while to convince the chief that it would be in his own best interests to see that Councilman Beitlinger remained behind bars until it was time for him to stand trial. Otherwise both Dorn and Beitlinger—and perhaps a fair number of other town officials—would find their pale and pimply asses in the federal lockup in Denver awaiting the sort of future that can make a man seriously depressed.

Once he was satisfied that Beitlinger was and would remain where he belonged, Longarm made his way back to Fat Ass Stella's whorehouse.

Nice woman, he was thinking as he went along enjoying the cold, crisp night air. Helpful too.

He lighted a Garcia y Garcia and stuffed his hands in his pockets as he walked.

Chapter 35

It was a good thing he'd hired the horse because the place he wanted was a good twenty miles or more down the Arkansas, and he was damned tired of walking. To say nothing of the time that would be required to walk that distance and then back again.

The road twisted and turned like a snake on hot coals, and his head was filled with the roar of the river the whole way down. Along about noontime he rounded yet another of the innumerable kinks in the well-traveled road, and broke out of the confining hills onto the beginnings of a broad sequence of meadows and flats that lay along the west side of the Arkansas.

Across the river the mountains were rugged and sere, but on the west or road side the hills receded and allowed the fertile bottomland to form an expanse of green so bright and pretty it damn near hurt a man's eyes to look at it. He hadn't seen grass this rich since he left Denver. No, come to think of it, he hadn't seen grass like this since the last time he got out of the city, out to where the farmers had taken up land and improved it.

This was almighty fine ground, and it didn't surprise him at all to see half a dozen or so cattle lying in the shade of some cottonwoods. When he got close enough, he realized that they were of some dairy breed. They had the high hipbones and hugely swollen, balloon-shaped udders that so often characterize dairy cows.

He had no idea what breed they were, but just looking at them, a body could tell that they were some sort of pureblooded stock. The cows were a pale tan in color, with cream-colored faces and huge, incredibly lovely eyes.

Longarm had heard more than one lovely belle pout and complain because the Good Lord above had chosen to give His prettiest eyes and longest, curliest eyelashes to a bunch of bony-faced cows instead of to them. Longarm didn't know about all that. But he would admit that there was nothing like a calf when it came to pretty eyes.

Off on the right side of the road he spotted the dead tree with a zigzag lightning scar on the trunk that he'd been told to look for, and immediately past it on his left was a lane leading toward the river and a small collection of sheds and outbuildings. There were probably half a dozen log buildings. And three towering haystacks that were fenced to keep critters away from them.

Longarm reined his rented nag into the lane. As he came nearer to the buildings he saw that one of them—and not the largest of them at that—wasn't an outbuilding but the house. It was a small, square cabin built of aspen and chinked with mud.

Aspen didn't last, and already it looked like the thin logs had warped enough to keep the owner busy rechinking the gaps. In another couple of years the cabin would have to be replaced. But for now the fellow was apparently making do with it as it was.

Longarm dragged the hard-mouthed horse to a stop in the yard between the house and the largest building, which from a distance he'd taken to be a barn, but could see now was an equipment shed instead. He could see haying machinery in there, a mower and a rake and a couple of skids. The building didn't look like all that much, but the machines were impeccably clean and gleamed with oil.

"Hello," he called out. "Is anybody home? Hello?"

About the time Longarm thought he would have to give up, a slender man wearing a Scotch cap and canvas gloves came out of one of the smaller sheds. He was holding a wickedly curved scythe in his hands. The scythe blade had an edge on it that was shiny from sharpening.

A tool like that could take a man's head clean off his shoulders with one sweep of the curved handle.

Longarm gave the scythe a long looking at before he nodded to the fellow holding it and stepped down from the horse. Just in case. He did not, after all, know how this livery stable nag would react if there happened to be gunshots and the smell of blood.

Longarm touched the brim of his Stetson politely and said, "H'lo, Mr. Campbell. I'm United States Deputy Marshal Custis Long. And I'd like to have a few words with you."

He had no idea what sort of reaction that news would bring. But he was ready. In case.

Chapter 36

Ellis lifted the scythe, and Longarm prepared to take the man down.

The man merely shifted the implement into his left hand while he thrust the right hand forward in greeting. "Long, you say? The one they call Longarm, right? I've heard about you, Marshal." He grinned. "I had some friends inside who knew you pretty well. What can I do for you?"

He shook Longarm's hand. There was no trickery. Just greeting. "Let me hang this thing back where it belongs, Marshal. Then come inside and we'll have a little something to drink." Ellis disappeared into his shed, and came back out a moment later without the scythe. If he was armed now, it wasn't with anything larger than a penknife. "Come along." He laughed. "Just don't expect anything fancy. I'm not much for housekeeping."

He was right enough about that. The interior of the little cabin was about as plain as plain gets. The walls were bare except for the horizontal streaks of dried mud chinking. There was a folding steel sheepherder's stove against the left side wall, and a bunk pegged into the right side wall. Some shelving at the back held some tinware, plates and cups and the like, along with various sacks and cans and bottles and boxes of foodstuffs.

A slab of bacon and a pair of hams dangled from a rafter. Pegs bored into the walls held a few articles of clothing. If Ellis owned a gun, it wasn't anywhere in sight. And there just weren't very many places in the cabin that could provide any sort of hiding place.

Ellis fetched two tin mugs from a shelf and brought a bottle with them. He dipped water into both mugs, taking it from a wooden bucket set beside the wood box, and poured small tots of whiskey from an unlabeled bottle.

"Here you go, Marshal." He lifted his mug in salute and said, "Mud in your eye."

Longarm tasted the whiskey. No wonder Ellis watered it down. It was worse stuff than Agnes Shreave served to her captive customers up on the mountain. Longarm smacked his lips in a display of pleasure and resolved to avoid allowing Ellis to give him a refill. "Thanks."

"Marshal, I've purely forgotten my manners. Sit down, please. Here." He dumped the firewood out of his wood box, set it on end, and offered that for Longarm to rest on. Ellis himself perched on the edge of his bunk. "What can I do for you, Marshal?"

"First thing, Charlie, you can call me Longarm."

The man grinned. "There's friends of mine I wish I could tell about having you say that to me."

"You don't keep up with the old crowd these days?"

"Naw. We don't have much in common anymore. You know how it is. You send men off to prison, you're gonna get a few who learn from the experience and change their ways because of it. The rest you're just sending to school, teaching them how to rob or con or strong-arm better the next time they have the chance. Never occurs to them, I guess, that the older and wiser fellas they're learning from weren't good enough to keep themselves out of the jug.

"But that won't change. And of course the simple truth is that prison does put a stop to crime." He grinned again. "But only while the man is inside. Once he gets out—

most go right back to what they were doing before or to bigger and better crimes." He clapped his hands and rocked backward. "Listen to me now, monopolizing the conversation and here you've come to ask me something. What is it I can do for you, Longarm?"

"First thing . . ." Longarm took a sip—a very small sip—of the vile whiskey and said, "You can tell me what you've been up to since you left Widow Shreave's inn."

"Oh, my, I'll be happy to tell you about that. I spent a lot of time up in those mountains, Longarm. Wasted time. I wanted to get rich. Wanted to do it honest and legal, but I wanted to get rich and that's the truth. Then I woke up one day and thought to myself, Charlie, you dumb son of a bitch, you've spent all this time climbing hills and breaking rocks and all you've got to show for it is some calluses. I will admit to you, Longarm, that when I looked at it that way, it seemed an awful stupid thing for a grown man to do.

"So I looked around to find something that I could get hold of for free or close to free but sell dear. Which, when you think about it, is pretty much what the whole idea of prospecting for gold is. You're trying to find something lying around on the ground that's valuable and other men will give you good money to get it.

"Fine idea, except I hadn't been finding much in the way of gold. Then I thought about these grass flats down here. I'd seen them from across the other side of the river, you see, when I'd be roving around prospecting those mountains. I'd seen this grass all green and pretty in the distance.

"And it came to me, Longarm, that Mrs. Shreave and Horace Barton are all the time grumbling at the cost of bringing hay and grain up into the mountains. Then I came down to Leadville and discovered that the mine owners and livery operators were complaining about the same thing. There just isn't any feed grown up there. It all has to be carried in, and the transportation charges are simply awful. Are you starting to get the idea now?"

Longarm laughed and said, "Indeed, Charlie, I think I am."

"I only had a little money after all my prospecting, but it was enough. I sold my rock picks and gold pans and gun and everything to raise a little capital. Took up land here along the river—nobody else wanted it, mind—and paid the fees on a little bit more. I already had an ax and Swedish bow saw, and I bought myself that scythe I was sharpening when you rode up. Bought that and the best whetstone I could find. And I went to mowing hay.

"Up this high you can only count on one hay crop a year, but that's enough. The mines and liveries in Leadville were so eager to buy my hay, they were bidding against each other for the privilege of paying me. And I didn't even have to haul it to them. They were willing to send their wagons down here to pick it up. All I had to do was to mow and stack it, and that I could do with no more investment than some sweat.

"Now, well, you can see how I'm doing. Got my mowing equipment out there. It's all paid for. And I'm planning for the future. There's a railroad building this way, up the Arkansas valley from Canon City, and another they say will come through Fairplay and down Trout Creek Pass. I figure once the railroads get to Leadville, that will end my edge when it comes to hay."

"Which is why you bought the cows," Longarm put in, seeing the direction Ellis's plans seemed to be going.

Ellis laughed again. "Exactly. I bought those Brown Swiss cows just a couple weeks ago. By the time my hay loses value as hay, I'll be using it to make milk and butter and sweet cream that all those miners in Leadville will be starved for. Are already starved for. And my milk will be fresh. Nobody will be able to bring it in by rail from down on the plains and begin to compare with me for quality." The little man with the big ears smiled. "I found my gold mine, Longarm, and this is it."

"I'm pleased for you, Charlie. I, uh, don't suppose you

162

know anything about the mail robberies up on the Mosquito Pass road."

"I've heard they happened. Say, you don't think I had anything to . . . you *do*, don't you? You think I could be the fella that's been robbing Ed and that killed that postal inspector. What was his name again?"

"Barrington," Longarm said. "Fitz Barrington. Did you know him, Charlie? Was he involved in your robbery those years ago?"

"I didn't know him, Longarm. But I can see why you'd ask. I said some stupid things to that judge when he sent me away. But that was just bluster and bullshit. Oh, I'm sure I meant it at the time. Hell, I probably would've done something to the man that day if I could have. But I got over that stupidity twenty years ago." He hesitated, then said, "Okay, not twenty. But at least twelve, fifteen years ago. I grew up inside those walls, Longarm. I don't recommend that method, exactly, but it sure worked for me. I don't figure to go back there. Even if I was to lose everything I've got here, I wouldn't try and recover that way. I'd just pick myself up and brush my britches and go on again."

Longarm nodded. "Just for the record, can you tell me where you were the first Tuesday of last month?"

"Hell, I dunno. Here, most likely. I went down to Pueblo, let me see, that would've been the second week. Went down and met the man who was delivering my cows. But that was after the date you're thinking of." He shook his head. "I don't guess I have any sort of alibi, Marshal. I haven't been up on that mountain since the day I left Shreave's and gave up prospecting. But there's no way in hell I could ever prove that in a court of law." His sigh was long and sorrowful. "Are you gonna take me in for questioning and . . . you know?"

"No, Charlie, I'm not gonna do that. For one thing, you have some good friends in this country. People who vouch for you. For another thing, I believe you. I hope to hell you don't prove me wrong about that, Charlie. But I believe you."

And he did. Dammit. He'd had only two decent suspects to choose from, Charlie Ellis and John Smith. And he believed each one of them when they claimed to be innocent of the robberies and the murder.

Dammit.

"Tell me something, Charlie."

"If I can, sure."

"You've been to prob'ly the best school in the country when it comes to robbing and killing. How would you go about setting up to rob Ed Macklin?"

Ellis thought about that for several minutes. Finally he drained the last of his whiskey and said, "I wouldn't want to be seen, of course. So I'd want to know something about who else might be on the road. And I'd want to know when and where to expect Ed. I mean, it's obvious where he's gonna be. But not exactly when he'll be there. You know?"

Longarm nodded.

"So I'd want to find a vantage point where I could see a good bit of the road above and below. Then I'd just sit there and let Ed come to me."

"That's pretty much the way the robber has been doing it," Longarm said.

"Of course."

"Then why would he've killed Barrington?"

"I'd guess the robber did or said something so that Barrington could identify him. If he did that, the robber would figure he had no choice. It'd be Barrington or him. No question which he'd choose if it came to that. It'd be *ker-pow*. Pop Barrington one between the horns, nice and clean. Then get the hell away from there."

Longarm grunted. What Charlie Ellis suggested was very much the same thing John Smith had described. The killer and Fitz Barrington had words. Then Barrington died. Just like Ellis said. *Ker-pow*. Right between the horns and away from there.

"There's something—" He didn't finish the statement. Didn't know how to. But there *was* something nagging and gnawing at him. Something in the things Ed Macklin and John Smith and now Charlie Ellis had all told him.

If he could just figure out what the hell that something was. . . .

Chapter 37

Whatever that thought was, it just wouldn't come clear to him, although he pondered the various statements the whole way back up the Arkansas valley. At the foot of the Mosquito Pass road he turned east, leaving the river behind and below him.

From there the going was agonizingly slow. Whenever the road gained elevation at a rate of more than one foot in a hundred or so, the livery nag wheezed and staggered and acted like it could barely lift one foot in front of the other. Most of the time Longarm thought it would be quicker if he got off and carried the horse instead of doing it this way. Still, Custis Long was a traditionalist when it came to things like who wore the saddle, so he stayed on top. The method was slow. But more dignified than the alternative.

He did eventually reach Barton's. And got something of a horse laugh from a trio of mule skinners who were taking a string of thirty-odd stout Missouri mules across carrying crates of tools and mining equipment that were being shifted from a dying mine in Alma to a more productive one in Leadville.

"At least your horse is useful," one of them said. "Grilled over low coals'd be tasty."

Longarm sighed. And offered to buy the mule skinners a drink. He couldn't object to their fun-making. Hell, it was true. About the only thing that'd prevented him from making lunch of the poor creature was that he'd have to pay for it if he failed to return it.

He got a good night's sleep that night—without getting in line for a visit with the fat little Ute girl, thank you—and left early the next morning for Shreave's, where he expected to meet Ed Macklin.

The next question would be if Longarm's bait would attract any flies. Or in this case, robbers.

When they'd met last week on Macklin's return trip to Alma, Longarm had advised the letter carrier to do some bragging. Loud and long. His story was that this time he'd fooled the Mosquito Pass robber by leaving all the valuable mail behind, it being the first carry of the month and apt to be stolen.

Longarm's idea was that if this news reached the robber, the man would be tempted into a second try this month.

And this time Longarm would be there when the robbery happened, not traipsing about on a wild-goose chase in the mountains.

He reached the pass a little short of noon—could likely have made it sooner if he'd been on foot—and couldn't help feeling a tightness in his spine at the thought that up there on the south side of the pass, Sharpshooter John Smith might well be looking at him through the sights of an old but damn-all accurate sniper's rifle.

Longarm didn't see him. But then he wouldn't. And if Smith was there, he offered no indication of it. Longarm rode on through, the faintly creepy sensation of being spied upon disappearing once he was clear of the pass and on his way back down to Shreave's Inn, where there would be poor food, lousy whiskey, and lusty companions available.

One out of three ain't bad, he considered.

Chapter 38

"G'wan." He slapped Betty on the ass—pretty nice ass, actually—and gave the naked girl a nudge toward the fireplace. "I want to get some sleep tonight. Macklin's leaving at first light, and I want to be fresh and fit if I'm gonna sneak along behind him."

She made a pouting face, but again he gave her a gentle push away from the side of the rumpled and sweaty bed where, for the past hour, Longarm had been playing slap-and-tickle with her.

"Go on now, honey. I'll be back tomorrow night if everything goes all right."

"You promise?"

"Sure I do," he lied.

"All right then. But mind you made me a promise. And mind it's me you'll pleasure again t'morra night. Don't you be letting Lou in ahead of me."

"Just you," he assured her. Well, unless Lou got there first, of course. "Go on now, honey."

With a sigh Betty gathered up her clothes and slipped out through the fireplace. A few moments later he saw the red flicker and then yellow glow that indicated the fire had been rebuilt.

Just fine, he thought, lying back and lacing his hands

behind his neck. Everything seemed to be in place. Including spreading the idea that Macklin would be leaving the inn at dawn.

Out in the common room the letter carrier would be, oh, so casually mentioning that same thing, which Longarm had worked into several conversations too.

They hadn't been quite so obvious about planting the idea that Deputy Long would be trailing him in much the same way that Fitz Barrington had. But they'd tried to convey that impression without coming right out and making a formal announcement about it.

After all, criminals by nature are stupid, but even the dumbest crook would smell a rat if signs were posted and handbills printed.

Instead of preparing himself to follow Macklin, though, Longarm lay where he was for half an hour or so, dozing but not allowing himself to fall into sleep. Then, very quietly, he got up and dressed, except for his boots, which he set aside while remaining in his socks alone.

He didn't really expect anyone but the Shreaves to have access to that fireplace joining his bedroom with Agnes's. But a little caution never hurt. With that in mind, he used his saddlebags and a couple of spare blankets to build a dummy figure under the bedcovers, and wrapped a black bandanna around a head-sized wad of dirty clothes to place on the pillow.

The ruse wouldn't stand close inspection. But it ought to fool anyone who happened to peep in from the other side of the fireplace or who took a look from the hall door.

Then, with boots and Winchester in hand, Longarm crept out into the hallway and on into the cold, mountain night.

Ed Macklin would be leaving at dawn just as advertised, the reason being that Longarm wanted to have full vision to help keep track of him. Surveillance in the dark required very close contact, and Longarm did not want limited visibility to dictate where he had to be this day.

Of course Longarm would *not* be sneaking along behind Macklin the way Barrington had. Rather, he would precede the letter carrier by climbing from switchback to switchback. It was a notion given to him by the robber himself, who last week had come climbing onto the road huffing and puffing. No reason Longarm couldn't copy a page from the killer's book in order to catch the son of a bitch.

He slipped outside well short of midnight and put his boots on, leaving behind the inn, where he could hear someone busying about in the kitchen, presumably Agnes Shreave already at work preparing biscuits for tomorrow's breakfast. Women's work was hard, Longarm reflected, and never ending.

Not that he was in danger of running out of work to be done either. It was a sad truth that there would always be some greedy asshole willing to steal and kill and break the laws of man and God.

No, Custis Long and his fellow peace officers were not going to run out of work that needed doing. Although he wished someday they would.

He hiked his coat collar high and paid attention to the climb that would put him a couple of switchbacks above the inn.

Chapter 39

Son of a *bitch*! It was far short of dawn, so he was sure it wasn't Ed Macklin passing below him on the road. Instead it was a rather stocky figure who walked—how had Smith put it?—kinda fat.

Longarm's eyes had long since adjusted to the faint starlight, so he could see the shape of this nocturnal traveler, but there was not nearly enough light for him to make out any features.

He could, however, see plain as a turd in a punchbowl that this man on the road was carrying a shotgun propped on his shoulder. And he was wearing a dark slouch hat. Just like John Smith said the killer wore.

Without needing conscious thought on the subject, Longarm immediately abandoned his plan to precede Macklin's journey up the road. Instead he commenced shadowing this late-night traveler, taking care to make no noise.

A hard wind would've been nice to help cover any sounds he might make, but there wasn't any and Longarm didn't know how to go about conjuring one up. He'd have to settle for extreme caution. And hope for his luck to hold.

The man with the shotgun continued up the road just

as bold as brass for another three quarters of a mile or so. Then, considerably short of the summit, he just . . . disappeared.

Longarm didn't even see him go. It was that sudden. One second he was walking along the road, nearing a clump of stunted, twisted little cedars. The next second he was gone.

Had to've slid inside the cover of those cedars, Longarm realized. There simply was no other place he *could* be.

Longarm stopped where he was. He had been nervous enough trying to creep across hard soil and loose gravel while the robber—he was damned well convinced that this was his man—was walking too and making his own noises. Now, with the robber lying silent in one spot, there were no other sounds to cover Longarm's.

Longarm considered his position and the robber's. He needed to get closer, no question about it.

With a muted sigh Longarm crossed his fingers—he would've crossed his toes too if he could—and slipped out of his boots. Hard leather soles were too likely to be heard. Better to make this sneak in his socks and if the gravel hurt, well, that was tough. Some bumps and bruises down there would sure as hell beat a load of buckshot in the belly.

He carried his boots with him just as he had when he snuck out of the inn down below, and began the longest, slowest, quietest sneak he knew how to make.

Well before the first pale rays of morning light tipped the nearby peaks with yellow and gold, Longarm was in position. Taking another suggestion from John Smith's wealth of experience on this mountain, he'd chosen a patch of scrub oak to wriggle silently into.

Getting there without sound had been a bitch. The ground beneath the runty oaks was littered with the dry, dead leaves from countless autumns and a jackstraw puzzle of ancient twigs. He'd had to feel ahead of his progress

174

and clear the ground with care for every inch of movement. But he'd done it, and now he was exactly where he wanted to be, with his Winchester in hand and a good view of both the cedars where the robber was hiding and, just below that spot, the road where Ed Macklin soon would pass.

All he had to do now was to wait.

And to keep from scratching the insistent stinking itches that roamed all over him now that he had to hold still. It felt like he was lying in a nest of spiders, and the creepy-crawly feeling pestered the shit out of him. He steeled his resolve and lay there silently, motionlessly enduring the discomfort.

He heard Macklin a good four or five minutes before the letter carrier came into view. He could hear the steady, rhythmic crunch of footsteps as man and mule climbed the road both knew so very well.

Down beside the road the robber would be hearing these same sounds. Longarm wondered if the man's gut tightened at the thought of pulling off another clever robbery under the very nose of a United States deputy marshal. Surely he knew Longarm was supposed to be trailing Macklin today. After all, they'd gone to some trouble to make that clear.

Now if only the fish took the bait . . .

Macklin came into view and continued on, unaware that he was being watched by two pairs of eyes.

He walked clean past the cedars, and for a moment Longarm thought he'd somehow fucked up and missed the robber changing to another hiding point further up the mountain.

Then, when Macklin's back was presented to the cedars, the robber stepped out onto the road with a deliberate crackle and crunch to announce his presence. He was wearing a flour-sack hood now with holes for him to see out of, and was carrying the shotgun cocked and ready. It was an intimidating sight, no question about it.

Sure enough, Macklin heard the robber's noises. Stopped. Turned around.

Just as he'd done those other times before, the robber silently motioned with the muzzles of the shotgun.

Those tubes must've looked a foot and a half across to Ed Macklin's eyes. Longarm could see in the mailman's expression that bravery in the face of large-bore guns was not his strongest suit. The man was scared. Longarm didn't blame him. The more so since Macklin had already seen the damage this very shotgun was capable of inflicting on a human body. Barrington's body must have been an ugly thing to behold.

And now Ed Macklin was once again staring into those awful deliverers of death.

Not for long, though. Scared though he might be, Macklin wasn't rooted in place. If anything he was galvanized to speed.

He hurried to the mule and unstrapped the mail pouch that rode high on the pack frame. He held his hands high to make it clear to the robber that he wasn't going to try anything, and tipped the pouch off the far side of the mule. It hit the ground with a dull, heavy thump.

The robber motioned with the shotgun again, waving Macklin down the road and on about his route.

Macklin wasn't slow to comply. He grabbed up the lead rope of his patient mule and took off up the road as fast as he could yank the protesting mule along in his wake.

The robber barely gave him time enough to clear the immediate vicinity—after all, he was sure to know that Longarm was due to come along mighty soon—and grabbed up the pouch.

Or tried to.

The mail sack had been weighted with something other than envelopes.

Today it held seventy pounds or so of lead that'd been wrapped in cotton batting to keep it from making much noise when Macklin dropped it.

The robber felt the weight and, probably recognizing

his mistake, whirled frantically round and round with the shotgun held ready to shoot.

If only he had something to shoot at.

Without revealing his position, Longarm called out, "You're covered, mister. Drop the gun or I drop you. Your choice, but make up your mind quick. Otherwise I'll put a slug in your belly to make it up for you. Right about the same place your first barrel hit Fitz Barrington.

"So do it, mister. *Now!*"

The robber froze. Longarm took a bead on the man's gut. He hadn't been blowing smoke up the man's ass.

His finger began to tighten on the trigger.

Chapter 40

"No. Don't."

Jesus!

Longarm was so startled he damn near jerked the trigger and shot the robber by accident.

That was a woman's voice behind the hood.

The robber—the woman—brought the scattergun's hammers down to half cock rather than risk a discharge when the gun hit the ground, then dropped it muzzle-down onto the road beside the phony mail pouch.

"Take the hat off. Then the hood," Longarm called out. "If you want to grab for a hideout gun feel free."

He knew, though, the features that would be revealed. And he understood now the same thing Fitz Barrington obviously had. When Agnes Shreave spoke she gave herself away. Now to Longarm. Then to Barrington.

The difference was that then the discovery had cost a man his life. The postmaster's kiss-ass postal inspectors weren't much when it came to detection or enforcement. But they didn't deserve to be put to death just so a greedy old bitch like Agnes Shreave could avoid the prison sentence she so richly deserved.

And was gonna get starting right about now.

"Step away from the gun and hold your hands high."

She did as she was told.

Only then did Longarm rise into view from beneath the brittle branches of the scrub oaks.

He held the Winchester steady on Agnes as he picked his way carefully down to the road. It wouldn't exactly be a good idea to lose his footing and slide down on his ass. The shotgun was still loaded, and it wasn't so far away that she couldn't grab for it if she saw a chance.

And Longarm didn't for a second believe that this evil old woman wouldn't fill his gut with double-aught just like she'd done to Barrington. This was a cold-blooded piece of shit, he reminded himself as he got down to firm and level footing.

"Turn around and put your hands behind your back, Agnes." He held the Winchester steady in his right hand while with the left he fished a pair of handcuffs from his pocket. "I'd advise you to hold still until we've gone through the formalities. But you go ahead and do whatever you want," he said.

He took a step forward.

And froze as behind him he heard the crackle and snap of footsteps.

"I'll give you the same advice, honey lamb," another entirely familiar feminine voice said.

"Lou?"

"No, sweetheart, it's Betty." He heard a giggle. "I was coming back into your room this morning, dear. I wanted another poking with that pretty pole of yours. Imagine my surprise when all I found there was that silly dummy you'd made up."

"You knew what was going on, did you?"

"Of course I did, sweetie. We're a close family. I saw what you were up to and I hurried along. I wanted to catch up with Mama and tell her to stay hid. But, well, you see how it's turned out. Sorry about that, baby. You're a stud in the sack, dear, but not *that* good that I'd pick you over my own mama. Like I said, we're a real close family."

"A rich one too, eh?"

"Not yet, but we're getting richer. Mama, do you want me to shoot him or would you rather do it yourself?"

"You go ahead, honey," Agnes said.

Longarm heard the rather unpleasant sound—at least under these circumstances—of a pair of heavy hammers being brought to full cock.

Apparently a fondness for shotguns ran in the Shreave family.

He felt his blood go cold as he braced for the sound of the gunshot.

Chapter 41

What he heard was no explosion of gunpowder. Rather it was a dull, wet sound much like that of a cleaver thudding into a hunk of raw meat.

Agnes Shreave let out a shriek, and Longarm turned to see Betty Shreave's body hit the ground as limp and lifeless as a sack of corn.

Her girl's face had disappeared, and there was a thin sheen of bright red sprayed over the ground in front of where she'd been standing.

Longarm saw the body fall, and a moment later heard the boom of a large-bore rifle high on the mountainside.

He started to look up, to see if he could spot the smoke from the Sharpshooter's rifle.

A scrape of leather on gravel behind him served as a reminder that he wasn't alone here.

Longarm spun back around toward Agnes just in time to see the old bitch snatch up her shotgun and swing the muzzles toward his belly.

Son of a *bitch*, he had time to think.

He didn't need time to work out what he had to do, though.

Without any need for conscious thought Longarm tipped the barrel of his Winchester up—he still had hold of it in his right hand and was still holding the handcuffs in his left—and tripped the trigger.

A .44-40 slug the size of the first joint on a man's thumb slammed into Agnes Shreave's stomach, doubling her over and rather effectively removing any interest she might have had in using that scattergun.

She sat down in the road, falling backward onto the mail pouch with its load of useless lead. Her legs were splayed wide. It was a most unladylike posture, Longarm found himself thinking. But then there wasn't a whole hell of a lot about Agnes that was ladylike.

"You son of a bitch," she whispered.

"Drop the shotgun."

She didn't. But then she probably wasn't paying much attention right then to anything past her belt buckle.

He could have shot her again. Probably should have. He didn't. Instead he circled around behind her and reached past her shoulder to take the shotgun and pull it out of her hands. She didn't resist.

He let the hammers down again—damn old woman had had time to cock them; he'd been close this time—and tossed the gun to the side of the road. He could collect it later. Along with other things. Like Lou. He bet Lou would be lonely as the only Shreave in the penitentiary.

"Finish me, you bastard," Agnes whispered.

"No, I don't reckon I will," he told her.

"You've seen gutshot folks die. It's awful."

"Yep. Sure is," he agreed.

"Finish me. I'm begging you. Spare me all that hurting. Finish me now. Please."

"Go fuck yourself."

Agnes Shreave began to cry.

Longarm ignored her—she wasn't a threat any longer, not to anyone—and waited for John Smith to come down to the road to join him.

The old Sharpshooter had earned himself a parole from his "sentence," Longarm figured. Damned if this display of public service hadn't earned him at least that much.

He hoped Smith would be pleased with the reprieve.

184

Watch for

LONGARM AND THE NEVADA SLASHER

268th novel in the exciting LONGARM series
from Jove

Coming in March!

**Explore the exciting Old West with one
of the men who made it wild!**

J. R. ROBERTS
THE GUNSMITH